Sanity Clause

A Humorous Holiday Romance

R. Lee Procter

Black Rose Writing | Texas

©2023 by R. Lee Procter
All rights reserved. No part of this book may be reproduced, stored in a retrieval system or transmitted in any form or by any means without the prior written permission of the publishers, except by a reviewer who may quote brief passages in a review to be printed in a newspaper, magazine or journal.

The author grants the final approval for this literary material.

First printing

This is a work of fiction. Names, characters, businesses, places, events, and incidents are either the products of the author's imagination or used in a fictitious manner. Any resemblance to actual persons, living or dead, or actual events is purely coincidental.

ISBN: 978-1-68513-333-7
PUBLISHED BY BLACK ROSE WRITING
www.blackrosewriting.com

Printed in the United States of America
Suggested Retail Price (SRP) $18.95

Sanity Clause is printed in Book Antiqua

*As a planet-friendly publisher, Black Rose Writing does its best to eliminate unnecessary waste to reduce paper usage and energy costs, while never compromising the reading experience. As a result, the final word count vs. page count may not meet common expectations.

Sanity Clause

PART ONE

CHAPTER ONE

Mike Dillon was no multi-millionaire, that was for certain. I mean, would a multi-millionaire be dressed as he was, in a powder blue, grease-stained poly cotton work shirt, with filthy industrial cargo pants in non-matching khaki? And the shirt with a pair of embroidered emblems: "Mike" on one side, and "One-Stop Car Care" on the other? And the greasy 'gimme cap' that said "Sluggish Engines Love Bardahl?" Would any self-respecting moneybags be caught dead at the World Economic Forum in Davos dressed like this?

No, Mike Dillon was a beer-drinkin', truck-drivin' just plain Joe: a blue collar, salt-of-the-earth working stiff with a single thing on his mind: tonight he was going to propose to the girl of his dreams, the adorable Stacy Simmons. And he was going to pop the question at the site of their very first date: Bob's Burger Shack, where Mike had driven Stacy in her 2009 Ford Escape after One-Stop had fixed her rear motor mount. The Shack was adorned with decorative strings of blinking red and green Christmas lights as befit the season. Mike had his "anniversary" gift (this was the six-month anniversary of their first date) and he had his speech all memorized.

There she was, in "their" booth, right across from the all-you-can-drink fountain station. She'd obviously just come from the bookstore, because she was still dressed in her bright red sales apron. She waved at him with her usual giddy enthusiasm, then scooted out of the booth to give him a boa constrictor hug. "It's so good to see you!" she squealed. "How was your day, honey?"

"Great! Because I knew that tonight I'd be with you, sugar." Mike slid into the booth, and there it was in front of him: his favorite meal, the one he'd had every time he'd come here: Double Steakburger with cheese and bacon, waffle fries and Bob's signature Salted Caramel Milk Shake. A feast! "So…here. This is for you." He handed her the gift. She took it with one hand as she rummaged through her purse with the other.

"And this is for you, love. Let's open 'em together, okay?" They both tore open the packages, and they both gasped with wonder as they viewed their treasures. "Oh, Mike!" Mike smiled as Stacy opened the gift box and swooned with pleasure at the Precious Moments porcelain Christmas ornament featuring two apple cheeked cherubs with black teardrop eyes hugging each other as they held a cherry red heart that said "I Wuv You."

Stacy nodded at Mike, who opened his gift. He gasped: a personal grooming kit! Comb, scissors AND a nail file, in a zipped canvas case. Mike took Stacy's hands and kissed them, then leaned back and tucked into the feast laid out before him.

They shared small talk over the meal, and as Mike slurped the last of his (scrumptious) shake, he got serious. He took a deep breath and clocked the moment: bustling restaurant full of festive diners, "Jingle Bell Rock" on the sound system, and directly before him, Stacy's perfect oval of a face, (bleached) blonde bangs, genial mouth, and sparkling green eyes. "Stacy, I…that is, these last six months…well, I've never been so happy, I'm sure you know that."

"I do. I feel the same way. It's been, well, wonderful," said Stacy.

She put her hands back out, and Mike took them. He looked into her eyes. "I never thought I'd find someone…I mean, look at me! I'm nothing special, just a run of the mill grease monkey. Why would any woman ever go for me? Especially one as, well, special as you?"

"Oh, Mike. It's not what you do. It's who you are! How many times do I have to tell you that!"

"A lot, I guess." They both laughed. "Anyway, I…that is, I've got a question to ask you. It's something I've been thinking about for so darn long, and, well…" He broke off eye contact and looked down at the table.

"Don't be afraid, Mike. Say it. Say what's in your heart."

Mike raised his head again. "Stacy…what I want to know is…why are you taping this conversation?"

Stacy opened her mouth to say, "YES!" but then froze. Her face fell, and she cocked her head at Mike. "What…did you just say?"

"I asked why you're taping this conversation. You're taping it, and the woman in the baggy blue sweater two tables over is videotaping it."

Stacy pulled her hands back and feigned astonishment. "Mike, have you lost your mind? That is THE most bizarre…"

Looking straight at her, he pulled a black device the size of a business card out of his pocket and held it up. Tiny silver letters said "D-TECHTR9HX." Two lights on top, red and green. The green was lit.

Stacy's eyes went wide as her mouth dropped. "That's…you can't…no way. That's spook stuff, Mike. Top secret CIA. NOBODY has those."

Mike's smile was not quite a smirk. "Why Stacy, how would a simple clerk at a Podunk bookstore possibly know that?" They both heard a loud, "HEY!" and a younger man in dark glasses – slim, late 20s, dressed in all black business casual – dropped some eyeglasses in front of Mike. "You were right, boss. Lipstick cam." The owner of the glasses, a feisty brunette in leopard-print yoga pants and a baggy blue sweatshirt, hustled over. The sweatshirt said, "Putting on Yoga Pants Counts as Exercise." She reached for the glasses, but Mike grabbed them, looked them over. "These are junk."

The brunette grabbed them. "Good enough to get lover boy on tape."

"Doing what, eating a hamburger?" said Mike, but he didn't really care, because he knew he was in the clear. He turned back to "Stacy." "So…can you turn that thing off now?" She took the smartphone out her purse, put it in front of her, flicked up the recording app and killed it. "Now," he said, "who are you, and how did you get to me?"

"Stacy" massaged her temples. Her shoulders slumped forward and she looked off toward the parking lot. "My name is Cheryl. Cheryl Brewster."

"Mike" held out his hand. "Magnus Diller. Of course you've known that since the first moment…actually, quite a bit before we met. So, Cheryl, tell me the whole sordid story."

Yoga Pants piped up, "What's it worth to ya?"

Magnus said, "What's your name?"

"Karen Creavey."

"Karen Creavey," said Magnus, "This is my associate, Dwayne Schofield. It's worth me not bringing the hammer down on both of you for stalking."

Cheryl pondered this. "Okay. So…the thing is, Karen and I have a kind of…I guess you'd call it a 'hobby.' We buy the 'Forbes 400' issue every year, then we try to figure out which of the wealthiest men in the world is worth, ummm…"

"Targeting?" said Magnus.

"Researching," said Cheryl. "The more we looked into you, the more interesting you got. So secretive! You were the only one Forbes didn't have a picture of."

"We figured you might be hiding something," said Karen.

"Yeah, I was hiding from people like you. Go on," said Magnus.

"Well, Karen has a friend who has a friend who knows somebody that's a data specialist at the FBI, and the FEEBS came up with the one extant photo of you."

Karen said, "Dover Point High School? Senior class? 1968?"

Magnus gave Dwayne a sullen glance. *How the hell did we miss that?* Then he turned back to Cheryl. She said, "Karen has some proprietary software that searched the Internet for a match. Imagine our surprise…and shock…when a guy who looked just like that younger guy only aged up 50 years turned up on OK Cupid!"

"So, what was the deal with that?" asked Karen.

"None of your business," said Magnus. He turned back to Cheryl. "So your play was, what, hot romance, marriage proposal, and then…

"A quick settlement," she said. "Low seven figures. We're not greedy."

"No, of course not." Magnus took another mental snapshot of "their" burger joint. This was the last time he'd go slumming in this pathetic little dump. Thinning crowd, a pitiful little silver tinsel Christmas tree, and Burl Ives singing "Holly Jolly Christmas." "Well," said Magnus, "thanks for playing, 'Stacy.'" He shoved the 'Precious Moments' ornament toward her. "Don't forget your gift, so we can remember all the 'Precious Moments' we spent together."

CHAPTER TWO

Magnus was sprawled in the backseat of his sweet, sweet cobalt blue BMW M6 convertible: the last of the best, just like him. 4.4-liter M TwinPower Turbo V-8, 552 roaring horses: a Chariot of the Gods. What Magnus liked about this particular BMW was that it *wasn't* a Rolls or a Bentley. People stared at those. They noticed who drove them, judged them. 'Another scumbag Boomer having a mid-life crisis.' But this beauty? Nothing to see, just another dreamboat with a double-kidney grill. All the ridiculous opulence of the Brit-mobiles with none of the rubbernecker hassle. And with a ragtop! So he could stare at the beautiful blue sky, like he was doing right this very moment. He lifted the frosty bottle of Dom Pérignon and took his third giant gulp.

Dwayne was at the wheel. "So, genius," said Magnus, "Ready to settle our bet?"

"Sure, why not?"

"You bet me..." said Magnus, savoring his triumph, "...that I could find true love – real, authentic love – if I hid my identity and posed as an average joe."

"I did indeed. I think I'd had too many margaritas."

Magnus could feel that warm, wonderful 'click' as the champagne endorphinized his hungry brain. "We did everything by the book, did we not?"

"We did," said Dwayne.

Magnus knew he was rubbing it in, but he just couldn't help himself. "We created a whole new identity: driver's license, Social Security card, passport, library card..."

"Yep," said Dwayne. He knew this was coming, and he was humoring the old man.

"We bought that car repair shop through a cut-out."

"Handled it myself," said Dwayne.

"Rented that sad little apartment, bought that godawful 1999 rust-bucket Chevy Silverado, with the ripped upholstery and the broken radio..."

"Cheap, though," said Dwayne.

"We did everything according to your rules," said Magnus. "And the "OK Cupid" profile?

Perfection. Mike Dillon wasn't a loser, but clearly a, oh what would you call him…"

"A sad sack," said Dwayne.

"Yes, right. And then Stacy…"

"You mean Cheryl?" said Dwayne.

"Cheryl, right…" He took another belt of champagne. So wonderful. So what if he wouldn't be able to stand up when he got back to the compound? "…Cheryl pinged me. And you thought she might be legit."

"Why not?" said Dwayne.

"Because we'd been up live on the website for six weeks and she was the very first one who showed any interest? I saw the words 'gold-digger' flashing in neon lights."

"You did indeed, Boss. Told me there's no way anyone with money can ever find true love because the money always gets in the way."

"More than that, Dwayne. I said that there's no such thing as love anyway, that even amongst the great mass of yahoomanity it's all 'Let's Make a Deal.' And I was right."

"You were right, boss."

"Damn right I was right."

"When you're right, you're right. Hell, even when you're wrong, you're right."

Magnus had to think about this for a moment. Was Dwayne being sarcastic? Whatever. "Okay, then. Pay up."

Left hand on the steering wheel, Dwayne slid his right hand into his pocket and dug out his wallet. He handed Magnus a single dollar bill. Magnus took it and tucked it into has greasy khakis. He took one last swig and, right out of nowhere, he felt a tremor in his chest. Was it…could it really be…sadness? Regret? Was the booze making him maudlin? He suddenly saw Stacy's face the night they had that picnic in Memorial Park: hot dogs and potato salad, with cupcakes for dessert. A free concert with six duffers playing Dixieland jazz under the stars, and at the very end, when she kissed him…well, he never really thought it was love, but for just that one moment, it *felt* like it *might be* love. His whole body shivered with pleasure at the memory. And in the very next moment, the awful truth. Magnus realized he'd never feel anything like that ever again. And it made him want to weep.

CHAPTER THREE

Magnus loved everything about the executive headquarters of "Opportunity Investments." He ran his real estate empire from a cluster of beige offices on the third floor of the Shady Lane Office Park. Shady Lane was a fading, bone-tired concrete-and-glass mausoleum, left almost deserted by the twin trends of corporate downsizing and millennials leaving the 'burbs for "more dynamic urban centers." The rent was dirt cheap and no one ever came snooping around.

He'd chosen the name "Opportunity Investments" carefully. He wanted to hit that perfect note of generic, credible banality without becoming *so* insipid someone might mistake it for a CIA front. The corporate logo was a capital "I" bisecting a capital "O." It was soporific, sure…but was it coma-inducing? He'd have to give it more thought.

Morning meeting with the "Brain Trust," gathered around the IKEA executive conference table ("BEKANT"). Magnus bought all his office furniture from IKEA for two reasons. First, it kept the staff from getting too complacent. They were disposable, just like the furniture he made them assemble themselves. Second, it fit in perfectly with the mediocre surroundings: another message to visitors to move on, nothing special going on here.

The Brain Trusters were gathered around the table: notepads, cellphones and Starbucks cups in front of them. He'd hired each one of them right out of the Residential Property Management Program of Ball State University, in Muncie, Indiana. No Ivy Leaguers for him, no sirree! He wanted kids who were ambitious, hungry, and saddled with staggering amounts of student debt so they'd work ridiculous hours for a beginner's paycheck in hopes of moving up the org chart. Not that they did, of course. Turnover (except for Dwayne, who had lasted five years) was 80% after one year, 100% after two. This year's crew consisted of Ashley (26), Samantha (26), Brandon (26), and Lauren (25). Magnus sat at the head of the table, Dwayne at his right. On his left was 73-year-old Fletcher Skowron, Magnus's lawyer and confidante for forty-plus years.

Magnus kicked it off. "As you know, this is it for the year. Christmas is in a week, and tomorrow I'll be on the bird, wheels up at 7 p.m." It was the BMW of corporate jets: a 2006 Gulfstream G550 he bought off a disgraced Veep at Bear Stearns the week after the company croaked in 2008, a straight-up steal at twelve million. "I will be out of pocket, nestled in my gold-plated bunker on my doomsday estate in North Island, New Zealand. I will be preparing for the end of the world with my fellow plutocrats, as far as humanly possible from all this Christmas bullshit. So last chance. Whaddaya got?"

"Just one item," said Dwayne. "The Palekaiko Resort deal in Kauai."

"Remind me," said Magnus. Of course he knew everything about the deal, he just wanted to see if the Brain Trusters were on top of it.

"Habsucht Bank lent us 630 million for the whole megillah: 3 hotels, condos, 36 holes of championship golf. Ten days ago, tropical storm Debby ripped through northern Kauai, took out Princeville and Hanalei."

"But we're in the south, right?" said Magnus. "Around, what…"

"Poipu Bay," he said.

"Right." Magnus turned to Lauren, the youngest of his acolytes: cute, eager, auburn hair in a blunt bob, wearing a black blouse framed by a dark gray power blazer, right out of a fashion mag. "So this is your love child, right? What's my move?"

Lauren's steady gaze was betrayed only by the nervous quaver in her voice. "It's all good, Sir. I called the bank, spoke with Werner von Moltke personally. He told me to say hello." Magnus flicked it away. "He said they saw no reason to change the loan terms in any way. I did what you advised about being assertive, pressing for every advantage. I told him the storm would almost certainly lead to supply chain issues, affecting the ability of OI to meet our deadlines. We went back and forth for a couple of hours. So, ummm, I'm happy to report that Habsucht Bank has agreed to extend the loan terms for six months. That's 630 million dollars in our bank account, interest free as we commence building." She smiled eagerly at her boss.

Magnus turned to Dwayne. "So, genius, is that the right move? Are we good?"

Dwayne canted his head and stared right at Lauren, ice cold. Not mean, but deadly. "The tropical storm was an act of God. OI should invoke the "Force Majeure" clause in the loan agreement, bank the 630 million, shut down the resort plan, and resell the land for the two hundred million we paid plus another, I don't know, let's say forty million. That's 870 million dollars right to the bottom line, screw the bank, good for us."

Lauren looked stricken. She opened her mouth as she looked from Dwayne to Magnus, and then at the other Brain Trusters, who had taken a sudden interest in the imaginary imperfections in the laminated plywood table surface. "But…no, this isn't right. I mean, ummm, the storm didn't come within thirty miles of us. We can't just…"

Magnus took over. "Oh yes we can, Lauren. It's not about what's right, it's about what we can get away with."

Magnus wondered if Lauren would fold, and he was happy she didn't. She was a fighter. "With all due respect, Sir, I was pushing it already. We suffered no damage. There's no way that bank is going to let you…"

Magnus erupted with well-practiced fury. "IT'S MY MONEY, DAMMIT! THAT'S WHY I'VE GOT LAWYERS!"

He turned to Fletcher, who gave him a nod. Fletcher then turned to Lauren. "The bank will sue us, you betcha. We'll counter-sue. That's the first five years. We'll probably lose, so then we'll appeal. Lose, appeal, lose, appeal: another seven, maybe eight years. That's TWELVE PLUS YEARS of interest on their 630 million, plus the interest on the 240 we make by selling the land. After a while, the bank will either give up or they'll trash us in the financial press, at which point we'll sue then for libel for three billion dollars."

"And eventually," said Magnus, "they'll beg us to keep the 630 million just to get rid of us."

Lauren sat there, mouth agape. All the other Brain Trusters edged away from her as if she'd suddenly come down with smallpox.

Magnus fixed her with what he thought of as "the laser." "Lauren, you're a very nice girl."

"Th-thank you," she said, near tears.

"I meant that as an insult. I'm afraid I misjudged you. You're far too nice to work for me. What I'm looking for is…" He turned to Dwayne. "…stone cold killers, like this young genius right here. See, you think 'fairness' is a thing. It's not. Now WINNING, that's a thing. In fact, it's the ONLY thing. We win, they lose. We get everything, they get nothing. Nothing." He turned to the other Brain Trusters. "Anybody else here think there are (air quotes) 'rules' that we're supposed to care about?" The tiniest of head shakes from wide-eyed heads on rigid bodies. Magnus turned back to Lauren. "You're a loser. You're fired. Pick up your stuff and get out."

She was stifling a sob, struggling to hold it together. She picked up her leather padfolio – the one she'd purchased as a gift to herself for getting this awesome new job – and trudged from the room like a death row prisoner on the Last Mile. Everyone stared at her as she disappeared. Then all eyes turned to Magnus. He knew in a blink he'd nailed it, as always. *They're mine.*

"Okay, then," said Magnus, "Samantha? You're in charge of the Palekaiko deal. Questions?" She swiveled her head 'no.' "Good. Get it done. Any trouble, talk to Fletcher. Anything else? Two weeks out of pocket, this is it, people." Ashley meekly half-raised her hand. "What?"

"I was…that is, a couple of us were wondering if there'd be any kind of, you know, like, company Christmas party? Get-together? Whatever?"

Magnus grimaced. "The Opportunity Investments Christmas party is you going after work to your favorite Mexican restaurant and having two beers that you pay for yourself. If there's nothing else, I'm outta here. See you in two weeks but that doesn't mean you can goof off. I'll examine your work product when I get back very, very carefully, got it?" Every head snapped up and down. Magnus was a happy boy, even if his face didn't show it. A flawless performance.

CHAPTER FOUR

Magnus was standing in Dwayne's closet-sized office packing the last items – cellphone charger, Viagra, Kindle Paperwhite – into his travel bag as Dwayne arrived holding a manila folder. He shut the door as Magnus nodded at him. "You're in charge, genius. Try not to burn the place down."

"Will do, boss. Have a great time. Are you meeting…"

Magnus grinned. "Betsey. She's already there."

"Betsey…aka Miss Brandi Foxx. With two x's. The pole dancer."

With the utmost gravity, Magnus enlightened his acolyte. "Ms. Foxx, with two x's, is the three-time winner of the Sparks, Nevada Pole-A-Palooza World Pole Dancing Competition. You know why she choose me out of all the horny chumps at the Itchy Kitty that night we met?"

"The size of your enormous, ummm….bank-roll?"

Magnus laughed, then held up his wristwatch. "This. Look, my smartphone can give me the time, but this baby…they call this 'The Legend.' 18 karat gold Rolex Daytona, one of three in the world. I could sell this on Ebay tomorrow for three million bucks. Brandi saw this, and knew, she just KNEW." He saw Dwayne shake his head. "What?"

"Look, I envy you. Two weeks of…"

"Good mischief."

"Right. But aren't you worried…I mean, you're so obsessed with flying under the cultural radar, what's to keep Brandi…"

"Betsey."

"…Betsey from selling her story to some cable sleazebag? Or writing a tell-all book, or streaming her own X-rated movie with Studd Lee Hungwell playing you?"

Magnus snorted. *He thinks I haven't figured this out.* "First, what's to tell? Pole dancer has sex with…who? Who the hell am I? Who cares? Second, she's being very, very well taken care of, as you yourself know. And all that cash is going into real estate developments hand-picked by me." Dwayne nodded. "And third, have you seen the non-disclosure agreement that Fletcher drew up?"

Dwayne smirked in admiration. "Okay, you win."

"Oh, and one more thing, genius. Let's say she goes rogue: leaves me, writes a scorching tell-all, breaches the agreement. There are worse things in the world than having a revered demi-goddess of this nation's Erotic-Industrial Complex advertise the sexual prowess of an insanely wealthy geezer like yours truly. I mean, if you're going to lose your anonymity, THAT'S the way to do it!"

"You win, boss. Oh, I almost forgot. I need your sig on this." Dwayne handed him the manila folder. Magnus skimmed it. "The mall deal," said Dwayne. "Here's the executive summary. The Chinese are ready to pull the trigger."

Magnus said, "Finally! Man, will I be glad to get this off my plate." His eyes skipped down the page. "Guangzhou Holding Company agrees to pay the sum of five hundred and fifty-two million U.S."… He looked up at Dwayne. "They met our price."

"That's right boss."

Magnus looked back at the contract. "Blah blah blah…at which time Guangzhou Holding will become sole owner of all eleven properties." He cocked his head at Dwayne. "Eleven? I thought the deal was for twelve."

"It was. But the deal stipulates that we have to provide documentation showing that all the malls have been profitable for the last five years. One of the malls is a dog. We cut that one out. We're going to get rid of it."

Magnus had zipped his travel bag, ready to leave. Instead, he plopped down behind Dwayne's IKEA (what else?) desk (MICKE). "Tell me about this 'dog.'"

Magnus noticed the split second mini-eye roll/snort: *"The boss is being a pain in the ass AGAIN."* Dwayne was getting better at concealing his disdain for the old man, but it still occasionally sparked up. Magnus knew that Dwayne thought of himself as Magnus 2.0, that someday (soon) he'd bolt this place to become a ga-zillionaire on his own. In fact, Magnus specifically chose Dwayne because he was smart, ambitious and a stone-cold killer, like him. But Dwayne was still a work in progress. He was patient: he knew he still had things he could learn from the old man. Magnus was the master of knowing when to fire people like Dwayne: the split-second before they knew enough to do him in.

"So…" said Dwayne, organizing his thoughts. "The dog. It's called the Towne Center Mall. First mall you ever bought, twenty-three years ago. Neighborhood went to hell, place was already in trouble when a ritzy new high-end shopping plaza opened seven miles away. Good-bye anchor stores. It's in a death spiral."

"And you know this how?" said Magnus.

"Tenants, the few we have left. Even the Mall Manager doesn't think we can make it. Told me he can't give away leases."

"And you're going to dump this place for how much?"

Another mini eyeroll, this one with a snort. *This guy can't let anything go.* "Not sure yet. I'm thinking seven-fifty, eight hundred thou. The mall is a tear down, somebody might want to clear it and put up a dollar store and some fast food places, or maybe condos."

"So. we're taking an eleven-million-dollar haircut."

Dwayne stood his ground, as Magnus knew he would. "Yes, we are. So we can cash a check for five hundred and fifty-two million, for a profit of sixty-eight million. And it gets us out of the mall business, which, as you told me, is tanking."

"Let me tell you a story. Can I, genius? It won't take long."

Dwayne shrugged. "Sure, please, go ahead."

Magnus bellowed, "FLETCHER!" Yes, he knew he could page Skowron through the intercom function on his phone, but – let's be honest – he loved screaming at people. Call it a perk. Fletcher peeked in the room. "Come in, I'm telling genius a story, I need a witness, you were there." Skowron nodded, took a seat. Magnus turned back to Dwayne. "First commercial property I ever bought," said Magnus, "was an old, beat-up apartment building, a hundred and ten units of sadness and despair. Everything was on the okey-doke until little shit started going wrong, like, oh, what?"

He looked at Skowron, who looked at Dwayne. "Electrical fires, rat infestations, flooding from clogged drains. We had a couple of break-ins, people mugged in the parking lot. Tenants started to move out."

"Then we get this low-ball offer for the place from a local realtor, and my gut tells me something's hinky." Magnus leaned back, staring at the beige ceiling tiles. He loved this part. "So I decide to go undercover as a maintenance guy, spend all day poking around. Well, I figure it out in two days. TWO DAYS!" Magnus paused. *Make him beg for the rest of it.*

"Soooo…" said Dwayne, "ummm…what did you figure out? What was the deal?"

Magnus waved at Skowron, who provided the punch line. "One of the biggest developers in the state was going to build a huge new business park. He had every parcel he needed but this one."

"The building manager was the so-called brains of the deal," said Magnus. "He was going to drive down the price, buy it for peanuts through a cut-out and then flip it to the developer for a sweet two-million-dollar profit. Well, guess who flipped one of his confederates, busted that scumbag and grabbed that two million for himself?"

"Ourselves," said Fletcher. "We were still partners then. And it was three million. Remember? At the last second?"

"Partners, right," said Magnus. *Was I really a 'partner' with that guy?* "And it was three million because I tacked on a 'don't screw with me' surcharge that the guy happily paid."

"Soooo…" said Dwayne, "bringing it back around to the mall deal. You think it's hinky? The fix is in?"

Dwayne was skeptical. Magnus pondered his response. How far did he want to push this? "My gut says yes."

"Your…gut. Uh huh."

Magnus was startled. Dwayne always backed the old man. Hadn't he made their deal clear when he hired him? 'Even when I'm wrong, I'm right.' "So you're the genius, genius. What's our move? Dump it and bank the sixty-eight million, or…

"Or what?" said Dwayne. "Or you cancel your holiday in New Zealand, ferret out these evildoers, and re-live a glorious triumph from your golden past?" Now Magnus leaned back and took a good look at Dwayne. The kid often gave him a hard time, but never about business, never in front of Fletcher, and never with this kind of naked derision. Dwayne sensed he'd gone a bit too far. "Look, this is a done deal. Just sign it, take 'yes' for an answer, have a blast in New Zealand. What's going on at this pissant mall, it doesn't make any difference."

"Oh, it makes a BIG difference, genius," said Magnus. "If we get taken and it gets around that we can be messed with, there'll be no end to it. EVERYBODY will do this to us." Magnus stared at Dwayne, who stared right back: not defiant, but resolute.

Fletcher finally broke up this glare-fest. "So, Magnus, I'm thinking you've got a case here, but it's not a slam dunk. Would you be willing to shave two days off your vacation to get this figured out?"

"Two days in Helltown?" said Dwayne, leaning in toward him, smiling. "Instead of snuggled in the loving arms of Miss Brandi Foxx? With two Xs?"

Magnus weighed his options. *Hell, sixty-eight million…but am I getting soft? You let shit like this slip by…then again, Brandi…the hot tub under the stars, champagne, those lips, those eyes, that hot, perfect body bathed in that thrilling perfume…* "Screw it, you win. Dump it, cash the check, we're done."

"Great," said Dwayne. "I'll have the final paperwork on your desk in, what…an hour? When are you outta here?"

"An hour is perfect." He looked at Fletcher, who nodded to him. "I just have one last item to button up."

CHAPTER FIVE

The office of Magnus Diller wasn't like the others at Opportunity Investments. The office of Magnus Diller was worthy of a Manhattan white-shoe three-name law firm: fireplace, book and trophy cases crafted from the finest oak, premium three hundred and sixty degree digital sound system, and a stupendous executive desk you could land aircraft on, with that old money walnut burl finish that Magnus loved. Cornelius Vanderbilt would have been right at home in this office. Yes, everything here was a thousand times better than that IKEA crap that the peasants had to endure, and that was the point. He was the Mighty Main Man with the Master Plan, the Indispensable Man, the Unitary Executive. Everyone else? Interchangeable parts. Don't get too comfortable, folks. He wrote the checks, they cashed them.

He eased into his ultra-plush mahogany arm-chair, upholstered in antiqued leather with brass nail trim and button tufting on the backrest. He'd actually rented "The Firm" and used the stop-motion function to make sure he was getting the one he wanted. Then he heard two very light taps on the door and said, "Come in."

Lauren cracked the door and peeked in. Magnus beckoned her to enter and pointed to one of the two plush burgundy chairs across from his desk. She tiptoed in, still in disgrace. As she sat, Magnus could see that she'd been crying. He handed her a tissue from the box on his desk. "Here you go."

"You-you wanted to see me, Sir?"

She clearly expected him to accuse her of stealing her desk stapler. Instead, Magnus vaulted up, maneuvered around the desk and plopped himself down in the plush chair right next to hers. He pulled an envelope out of his jacket pocket and handed it to her. "For you." She got that panicked look in her eyes: what fresh horror was this? What more could he possibly do to her? "Go ahead, open it."

Her eyes moved to the envelope, to him, then back to the envelope. She took it and pulled out a single sheet of heavy, cream-colored card stock. As she read, her eyes got wider and wider. When she was done, she looked at him in astonishment. (*He loved this part.)* "This is a letter of…of recommendation. I…I don't understand."

"This is your gold card for any job you want in this business, Lauren. Give 'em this and you're in. If anyone has any questions, have them call me. I'll do what I can to get you the job."

"Th-thank you. I'm…well, very surprised."

Magnus reached into the other inside jacket pocket and handed her a second envelope. She opened it and pulled out a check. "Oh my gawd,"she said. "Fifty…thousand…dollars." She turned to him, dumbstruck.

"Let me tell you a story, Lauren. About the very first job I had in this crazy business. What happened to you, in there, today? That happened to me. Got my head handed to me. My boss back then was…well, he was even more brutal than you think I am, if you can believe that. He wanted this piece of property for a housing development. It was owned by some folks who…well, let's just say they didn't have a sophisticated understanding of their rights under the law. He told me to make up a story to get them to sign away their rights to the property for nothing so we could evict them. The thing is, I knew these people. I'd gone to school with them. That was the point, they trusted me. I wanted to do it, but…I couldn't. And so he fired me just like I fired you, and then had somebody else decapitate the peasants. I was devastated. But, see, he gave me a letter just like this one and enough cash to get another job. He told me, 'Ya gotta toughen up, kid. There's two kinds of people in this business. Killers and losers. I hire killers. Now get the hell outta here and come back when you're a killer.'" Magnus reveled at the memory. Doing the gravelly voice of his boss – Hobart Pike, good ol' Hobie, the bastard – really brought back the moment.

"And…everything went okay after that?" said Lauren.

Magnus barked a single guffaw. "Next time I saw that bastard I was taking him down. Bought his company and kicked him to the curb."

"Wow. I understand. But…well, I'm not really sure I'm a killer."

"Oh, you can do it, Lauren." He smiled at her. *Listen up, this is the secret.* "All you have to do is make a resolution that henceforth you will do whatever it takes to succeed, and to hell with fairness. Really, that's it! There's no such thing as a 'fair fight.' There's winning, and there's losing. You want to be successful? To be like me? Then create a reputation for going too far. Make them fear you. You do that, you'll win before you even sit down at the negotiating table. And then you'll make the killer deal every single time." He leaned in just a bit and lowered his voice. "And remember. Always take it *all*, Lauren. Every single dollar. You don't win unless they lose, and I mean lose *everything*. No mercy. The harder you screw them, the more they'll fear you and the bigger your rep will get in the business." He stood. The meeting was over. They shook hands.

"Thank you, Sir."

"Good luck, Lauren. Let me know how you're doing."

CHAPTER SIX

Magnus walked back into the executive conference room where Dwayne, Fletcher and the Brain Trusters had gathered. He felt good in his "jet schlep" travel attire: charcoal double-brushed cotton hoodie over a comfort polo, khaki cargo shorts and boat shoes with no socks. He had his gear for the plane in a leather weekender duffel. "So where is it?"

Dwayne handed him the document. As Magnus looked it over, lovely Samantha, round face framed by a riot of red ringlets, asked, "Did you really go undercover to catch the people who were trying to steal five million dollars from you?" Magnus was startled for two reasons: that this story had become an office legend, and that the size of his booty had inflated.

Before he could answer, Dwayne chuckled and said, "That was a looooooooong time ago."

Magnus was miffed by this. *What was this kid doing to me?* He turned to Samantha and said, "Bet your ass. And I'll tell you why. I decided then and there, NOBODY screws me, even for one dollar."

Dwayne said, "Except this time."

This really set Magnus back. He could feel his jaw tighten. What the hell? He looked at Dwayne, who met his gaze. He had that little shit-eating smirk on his face. He liked it when Dwayne bantered with him, but never in front of the Brain Trusters, and never in a way that made him look bad.

"So," said Magnus to Dwayne, "You think I'm getting screwed."

"No, I don't," said Dwayne. "I think YOU think you're getting screwed. There's a difference." Magnus continued to lock eyes with him. "Look, boss, you're the one who has zero tolerance for getting screwed. It's just...I don't know...interesting to see you blow this off."

Magnus prided himself on his cool demeanor. He *never* got angry at work, especially in front of the worker bees, but now he could feel the blood rushing to his face. "So you think what? I should call off my vacation and go down there and spend Christmas super-sleuthing at a derelict shopping mall?"

"I do not!" said Dwayne, still with the smirk. "I think you should get on that bird and swill piña coladas and screw your…" He stopped himself just in time. "…bask in the attentions of your beloved for two lovely weeks. I just think you should be honest with yourself. About how you've changed. Because that means we've changed."

"I haven't changed."

"Hmmm. Interesting. Soooo…you think we're *not* getting screwed on this mall deal. Your golden gut is wrong, in this case."

For the first time in their professional relationship, Magnus felt like screaming "YOU'RE FIRED" at his best student and most valuable acolyte. "Just so I know," Magnus said to the Brain Trusters, "Give me the straight take. Are we getting screwed on this deal? Your best guess. Yes or no? You're no good to me if you aren't honest."

Nothing for half a minute, everyone remembering the fate of Lauren. Then, finally, Brandon went first. "No."

Then Ashley, then Samantha. Dwayne went last. "No. No. No."

After he answered, Dwayne looked at Fletcher. Fletcher was surprised by the challenge. Should he answer? Whose team was he on? But then Magnus nodded at him, and he finally said, "Nope."

Magnus stared back at Fletcher. "Fletch, put a seventy-two hour hold on the jet. Then get me to the Towne Center Mall with all due haste. Book me a room at the cheapest halfway decent business hotel you can find and call the Mall Manager. Tell him he's got a new…I don't know…maintenance guy? Security officer?"

"What about Santa Claus?" said Ashley. Everyone looked at her. She stammered, "Well, I mean, think about it." She looked at Magnus. "You want to spy on people, right? See what's really going on? If you're the shopping mall Santa, you'll be right in the middle of everything. You'll see every store, every customer…"

"Santa Claus!" said Magnus. "Tell the Mall Manager that…just tell him…tell him that 'corporate' is sending a new Santa down there, it's a favor, somebody knows somebody, blah blah, just let them wonder why, make it a big deal."

"Okay, then," said Dwayne. But Magnus wasn't going to let him off the hook that easily. If he was going to suffer, he was going to get payback.

"Let's make this interesting," said Magnus. "The current deal makes us sixty-eight million. If I'm right, that sixty-eight million goes right into my pocket. PLUS no one here gets a bonus this year or next, PLUS no vacation for anyone next year."

Brandon looked forlornly at Fletcher. "Can he even do that?"

"It's a bet. We're shoving our chips to the center of the table," said Magnus. "Just the way I like it. Winner take all."

"So. what's the 'lose big' part?" said Dwayne.

"You tell me, genius."

Dwayne thought it over. "If you're wrong and we win…let's see…we, the Brain Trusters, Fletch and myself, we split the sixty-eight million five ways." They looked at each other as this sank in. Thirteen million apiece, and change. In one week.

"The no vacation thing?" Brandon said quickly. "I'm good with it."

"And six weeks of vacation," said Dwayne. "And a trip of choice per person on the company jet." *Good for him*, thought Magnus. *Ask for too much. Make me afraid.*

"Okay, how 'bout this. You win, you get half the booty: thirty-four million split five ways, that's almost seven million apiece. Plus four weeks of vacation. No jet travel, the plane is mine."

Dwayne's face curled into that tiny smirk again. "You're the one who is always telling us that every negotiation is winner take all. It's a bet, boss. If you win, you take it all. If we win…well, I just think we should play by one set of rules. Your rules."

Magnus opened his mouth, but nothing came out. Dwayne had him. Those were, indeed, his rules. And Magnus was going to win, so it didn't make any difference anyway. "Ya got me, genius. Whoever wins, wins big, and whoever loses…"

"Gets nothing," said Dwayne. "So…deal?"

"Deal," said Magnus. He shook Dwayne's hand, and turned to Fletcher. "This," he said, "is going to be fun."

PART TWO

CHAPTER SEVEN

Mike Dillon was back! Mike/Magnus was wearing the man-of-the-people get-up he'd just purchased at Old Navy: an "everyday" black and red flannel shirt, baggy blue "comfort fit" chinos and – his best buy evah – a USA flag patch camouflage-pattern trucker hat. He was carrying an extra set of similar clothes along with his dopp kit in a careworn reusable grocery bag he'd found next to the store's dumpster.

The brassy, tobacco-chewing Uber driver didn't believe him when he told her he wanted to be dropped at the Towne Center Mall. "Are you kiddin'? That place is a dump! How 'bout if I take you to the Paradise Valley Shopping Plaza? Only be about a dollar more..." But no, it had to be the Towne Center Mall. As they cruised through town in the dinged-up, burnt orange Dodge Neon,

Magnus got a rare eyeful of urban blight. When they arrived, Magnus could see that his driver was being kind to the place. What the hell?? The Towne Center Mall would need about twenty million dollars of work to elevate itself into the 'dump' category. It was a wreck.

The Towne Center Mall was a perfect snapshot of the early 1980s, a decade not distinguished for its memorable architecture. In fact, it might have been designed by pre-Unification East Germans to discourage runaway capitalism. It was a fading fortress, a neo-brutalist citadel abandoned by a retreating army. This squatting gargoyle had no windows, of course: the whole point of these self-enclosed monstrosities was to cut people off from the real world and "immerse" them in a wonderland of retail.

The mocha-brown paint had faded to a sickly shade of splotchy mulberry, not having enjoyed a touch-up since the Clinton Administration. The kids who bought their Rubik's Cubes, Teddy Ruxpins and Cabbage Patch dolls here in the 80s had long since abandoned these melancholy shambles. Even as this realization dawned on him, Magnus thought, "*Shit. I OWN this place. This is mine.*" A horrifying realization lit up his brain: "*what if Dwayne was right?*" He suddenly felt as if he'd swallowed a cinder block. Then he fought back. "*No,*" he thought. "*Not possible. Trust your gut. You're right. Somebody nefarious did this. You can find them, turn this around. You can do this thing."* Still…once this was over, Magnus made a note to call the United States Department of Defense. If they needed a target for novice drone pilots to practice dropping heavy ordinance, he had just the place.

He ventured inside. Right away, he knew something was missing. What was it? Oh, yes: the thrum and bustle of busy shoppers. This place was so graveyard-still, he could hear every blessed "rum pa pa pum" of the ambient "Little Drummer Boy." *Was this place even open?* Well, the doors were unlocked…

He rounded the corner and entered the center court of the mall. At the far end, he could see a threadbare "SantaVille! Meet Santa At the North Pole" shanty. Santa was on a break, which was just as well because there were no kids around, and the resident elf was scrolling through posts on his smartphone. The mall was bookended by defunct anchor stores: Sears at one end, J.C. Penney at the other. Ex-Sears was a dark, forbidding tomb, and Ex-Penney's was adorned with a blizzard of yellow hazard tape as if a multiple homicide had occurred inside. Smack dab in the middle of the center court was the saddest Christmas tree Magnus had ever seen. Instead of spending the money for something magnificent, the manager of this mall had gone to a commercial lot and bought a fourteen-foot white pine that had already turned a shade of sickly brown. The decorations were an afterthought: white lights, red ornaments, and a sad smattering of tinsel.

Magnus strolled around the central court. Every extant enterprise was homemade and locally owned: the big national brands and franchise outlets had skedaddled. There was "Bodacious Books," a new/used bookstore fronted by a gigantic crate of dog-eared airport thrillers and bodice-ripping romance novels on sale for ten cents apiece. Then two empty stores – Florsheim Shoes, and a "Gadzooks" T-shirt shop – and then the "Munchkins Manor Toy Company," which seemed to be the kind of place Magnus loved as a kid: narrow aisles, shelves piled high with puzzles and board games, plus cheap novelty stuff like wax lips and whoopee cushions. Everything but customers, despite signage outside telling the world it was an "Official Santa-Approved Supplier for the North Pole!" Then finally the deceased "Dream Cloud Mattress Company." Something wrong here: the glass door in the entryway had been shattered, replaced by cracked plywood.

On the opposite side of the courtyard, "Grindhouse Coffee" had attracted three forlorn geezers caffeinating themselves at a table in the courtyard. Next to that – this was interesting – a business with *an actual line of customers*. Seven people, including three mothers with kids, were queued up to partake of the sweet wonders of "Cookie's Cookies."

He peered inside: a lively woman with silver-flecked brunette hair, clad in a red and green Christmas apron, was hustling about, serving her happy customers cookies and ringing up the sales. It was, by far, the cleanest, cheeriest, most popular store in the mall.

Then came a cluster of shabby storefront service providers squatting in what had been a jewelry store, a fashion boutique and a sporting goods store. The "Justice Done Legal Clinic" huddled next to the "NeighborCare Free Clinic," which abutted, "The First Storefront Church of Jesus Christ, Troublemaker." Of these three, only the Free Clinic had customers: three seniors waiting glumly for care by health care "experts" who were so downtrodden they couldn't find employment administering flu shots at a CVS.

Magnus decided to linger a bit. He wandered into Grindhouse Coffee and was greeted by a buoyant, avuncular man about his own age standing behind the counter. "Hello, friend," he said. "How can I make your day just a little bit better?"

"Well, a cup of coffee might do the trick."

"A cup of coffee?" said the counterman. "Why it just so happens I have a freshly brewed pot of that exact beverage." He poured some into a paper cup, popped a sippy lid on top and handed it to Magnus. "Here you go, my friend. Created by the cosmos for the sole purpose of enhancing your mood."

Magnus liked this guy. I mean, it was an act, but it was good, and it came from the heart. "Mike Dillon," he said, holding out his hand.

"Nick Van Ness. Business is a pleasure 'cuz pleasure is my business."

"How much do I owe you, Nick?"

"How much you got?"

"Sign up there says a medium coffee is a buck fifty."

"You got a buck fifty?"

"I do."

"Then it's a buck fifty." Magnus handed him two dollars and got back two quarters. He hated tipping but he was trying to make friends here so he put a quarter in the tip jar. "Thank you kindly, friend."

At that moment a geriatric African American man walked in clad in dirty sweats, shabby bedroom slippers and a camo-khaki 'woobie' jacket with the words, "When I Die I'll Go To Heaven Because I've Spent My Time In Hell: Vietnam 71-72" on the back. Nick drew him a coffee as he greeted him. "Darnell! Hardworking Mister Dynamite, in the house! And the coffee? That's *on* the house." Darnell gave Nick a sullen nod and walked over to the table, pulling out a Slim Jim snack stick. Nick looked at Darnell as he said to Magnus, "He's a regular. Gonna pay me back when he wins the lottery. Which is…"

"Tuesday!" said Darnell.

"Tuesday," said Nick. He turned back to Magnus. "Soooo…what brings you to this blighted playground?"

"I'm the new Santa Claus," said Magnus.

Before he could say another word, Nick shouted "COOKIE!"

Cookie, the cheery woman Magnus had seen serving her customers a moment ago, poked her head around the corner. "What?" She smiled at Magnus. "Hello."

"Hello," said Magnus. And he felt the tiniest spark of something. What was it? That feeling he'd had in the park with Stacy that night.

Nick said, "Can you…would you be so kind as to present the ceremonial Best Cookie on Earth to Mike here, to sanctify his reign as the new Santa of Townie?"

She disappeared for a moment, then came around the corner holding a chocolate chip cookie on a paper napkin. "Mike? We're happy you're here."

Magnus started to take a bite, but Nick yelled, "STOP!"

Magnus looked at him quizzically. "What?"

Nick looked him in the with profound mock-seriousness. "You can only make love for the first time *once*. Your first kiss, your first dance, your first child….and your first bite of the BEST chocolate chip cookie extant on the planet, in the galaxy, the cosmos. Are you ready for it? Are you ready to love a cookie more than you love…well…whatever you love most in this fallen world?"

Cookie was laughing. "Just eat the damn cookie!"

Nick continued to stare at Magnus. "Finally, Mike, are…you…ready to gain fifty pounds in a month? ARE YOU?"

Magnus said, "I'm ready."

Nick nodded, and Magnus took a bite of the cookie. His eyes widened. "Oh…my…gawd."

Nick cried out, "Ya see? YA SEE?"

Magnus stared at Cookie. "You made this?" She nodded shyly. "This is…is…amazing! This is absolutely the best…"

The air was split by an angry bark. "Mike Dillon?" Magnus turned and got his first glance at E. Gerald Dudley, Supervising Manager of the Towne Center Mall. "Follow me."

CHAPTER EIGHT

In E. Gerald Dudley, Magnus saw what his life would have been like had he not had the gumption to trample the rabble in the pursuit of his dreams. Dudley was an angry nothingburger pushing an empty suit through the air. As Magnus surveyed Dudley's tragic little office, he marveled at the man's whole-hearted embrace of his loser-dom. It was all of a piece, like an art installation: the scuffed double-bank steel tanker desk with the creaky Dell laptop used by four out of five losers, the industrial-beige fax machine *(they still had those??)* The Flowbee haircut, thrift-store (stained) necktie, the cheap-ass Casio F19-W wristwatch – the one favored by al-Qaeda terrorists, that could actually get you buried at Guantanamo Bay – I mean, was there a school for losers, where they taught you this stuff? Dudley picked up a fax. "Says here noon. You'd be here at noon."

"I was here at noon, I just got sidetracked scoping things out…"

"No scoping, just working," said Dudley. "Soooo….when did you graduate from Santa School?"

Magnus blinked. *Santa School?* "It was…oh, let's see…2017."

"You got your certificate?"

"Yeah, it's, ummm, in my stuff, back at the motel…"

"Bring it." Dudley buried his face in the fax.

"Really happy you're giving me this chance, Mr. Dudley." No reaction. "I, ummm, couldn't help noticing that there seem to be a lot of, you know, empty stores in this…"

Dudley's beet red face appeared as his fists jolted the Formica surface of the desk, sending the fax flying. "What POSSIBLE reason could you have to care about that? I'm working my butt off here, it's a damn miracle we're as booked as we are!" He scrutinized Magnus. "Are you a spy? You're from corporate, right? Yeah, that'd be about right. You're here to take me out, aren't you? I knew this would happen, KNEW IT! You want this damn job? WELL YOU CAN HAVE IT!"

"No!" said Magnus. "I'm not…I was just, ummm, trying to make conversation…"

"You listen to me, Mister" said Dudley, a worm-like purple vein throbbing in his forehead. "I'm holding this garbage dump together with duct tape and baling wire to make you bastards rich! You want to see what we're up against? HUH? DO YA??"

Magnus was cowering back in his chair. "Not really, I just…"

Dudley pounded away on his computer, then spun it toward Magnus. "Look at these pictures. I took 'em yesterday over at the goddamn Paradise goddamn Valley Shopping goddamn Plaza. That's fifteen minutes from here, Sluggo. Seven miles."

"Uh huh," said Magnus as Dudley waited for the chugging Dell to load the pictures.

"Okay," said Dudley. "Here's what we're up against." Dudley clicked through a series of smartphone snaps of a lavish, modern regional shopping destination, or, as the entry signage announced, "Your Luxury Shopping Resort." Magnus recognized the stores: these were the high-end, elite retailers his other malls featured. Plus elaborate fountains shooting arcs of water into the sky, a satellite gallery from the state's most prestigious art museum, and the kind of expense-account-friendly, celebrity chef-branded, foodie-fad restaurants he favored when he went to New York.

"I assume you saw our piece-of-crap Santa meet-and-greet when you were 'scoping things out,' right?" said Dudley.

"Uh huh," said Magnus

"Here's the competition. Ask yourself, where would you take your kid? Or better yet, we all know kids talk to kids, where would your kids likely demand you take them?"

(Magnus had never actually taken his kids to see Santa. The nannies had done that, then sent him the photos. He sometimes even looked at them.)

Now Dudley clicked through images of a lavish North Pole Christmas fantasy: really a pop-up mini-theme park devoted to the rapture of children. First, a giant walk-in igloo with an elaborate photo op with Frosty the Snowman. This amused the kiddies as they waited in the queue, where they were entertained by a quartet of perfectly costumed "Dickens Carolers," past a live reindeer petting zoo, and finally into a magnificent "Santa's North Pole Toy Workshop" filled with animatronic elves beavering away. And there was Santa, surrounded by comely female 'helpers' whose most important job was talking mom and dad into the thirty-dollar upcharge photo, with a candy cane holder that played "Santa Claus is Coming To Town" when it was opened.

There was more. After children ran down their wish lists for Santa and he nodded conspiratorially, they exited into an immersive mini-shopping mall. It was anchored by a thirty-foot-tall, wildly over-decorated Christmas tree that had a zillion presents underneath. It was full of high-end predatory retailers laser-focused on inspiring kids to torture their parents for This Year's Must-Have: American Girl, Disney, Lego, Build-A-Bear Workshop, Barbie and a "Fifty Top Toys" kiosk.

Dudley stared the screen, morose. "Appointment only. Twenty-five bucks a kid, plus thirty for the photo, and they've been booked solid for the last five weeks. They...are...printing...money over there." He turned to Magnus and glowered. "And you're getting up in my grill about *this place?*"

Magnus held his hands up in surrender. "I wasn't..."

Dudley said, "Maybe somebody in corporate loves you, but you're just another down-and-outer to me. You mess with me, it'll be the last mess you ever...it'll be...just don't mess with me, okay?"

"Okay!" said Magnus. "I won't."

"Damn right you won't. Now get out there and make those kids happy. Happy kids mean happy moms, happy moms spend money, and that means happy tenants. Now let me hear your "Ho Ho Ho.'"

This took Magnus by surprise. *Showtime. Damn.* He was seized by panic. "Ho, ho…uh…ho." Even Magnus knew how pathetic it was.

Dudley stared at him, horrified. "That's it? *That's* what they taught you in Santa School? And you *passed*?" Magnus nodded. "Try it again."

Magnus let the fright get the best of him. He bellowed, "HO HO HO!" in a loud, angry voice more suitable to the Big Bad Wolf.

Dudley stared at him, then buried his face in his hands. Magnus could just hear him muttering, "Oh gawd oh gawd oh gawd, why me, lord? Why?" Then he rubbed his face and, dejected, said, "Just…just get out there and do your best. Just…don't scare them, okay? Forget the 'ho ho ho,' just smile and listen and nod."

"R-right," said Magnus. He rose and headed out the door.

"One more thing," said Dudley. Magnus turned back. Dudley handed him his smartphone. He'd called up a blurry photo of a skinny teen in a hoody cruising the mall. "We got ourselves a homeless kid that thinks he lives here. Been trying to catch him for three weeks. If you see him, let me know. Catch him, there's 50 bucks in it for you."

CHAPTER NINE

Magnus changed into his Santa gear in the ram-shackle break room. The costume was wrinkled, ripped and soiled, and it smelled like damp sweat socks. The beard was sticky, which caused Magnus to ponder whether the last Santa might be, oh, say, an alcoholic flu victim. He didn't want to spend ten days in New Zealand flat on his back gargling chicken broth. He did the best he could with wet wipes on the beard and then gave up. He checked himself out in the warped full-length mirror under the word "SMILE!" Good enough, once he jerked up the pillow padding for his stomach. Show time!

"Oh, here comes Santa now!" Santa's "elf," a not-trying-to-hide-it gay twenty-something an-nounced his arrival to the forlorn line of parent-child customer pairs. As Magnus sat on the worn red velveteen mock-throne, the elf muttered in his ear, "I'm Sugar Plum. You're late."

"Sorry," said Magnus sotto voce, followed by a loud "HO HO HO!"

The elf drew back and winced. "Are you drunk?"

"No!" whispered Magnus, eyeballing the beady-eyed children and wondering what he'd gotten himself into.

"The last guy threw up on one of the kids," said Sugar Plum. "You ready? Who cares, we're on." He whirled and said in a cheery voice, "Okay! Who is our first lucky boy or girl?"

The first "lucky" boy was a tightly wound seven-year-old African American boy named Jamal. Before Magnus could ask what he wanted for Christmas, Jamal said, "You're not the real Santa."

"Yeah, I am too," said Magnus.

"Then why aren't you at the North Pole makin' toys? Christmas is in three days."

Magnus could feel his hackles rise. Who was this punk to question who he was? "Maybe I'm so smart I figured out a way to get done early. You ever think of that?"

This thing had gotten nasty in the first twenty seconds of his first kid. Sugar Plum tried to hand Jamal a tiny, cellophane-wrapped candy cane. "Why don't you tell Santa what you'd like for

Christmas?" Magnus caught the glare of the mother, shooting eye-lasers at him.

Jamal said, "A Braniac Junior Coding Robot."

Magnus wrinkled his brow. "A what?!?" Then he saw Jamal's mother frantically shaking her head NO!!!" Magnus, staring at her, said, "Well, Jamal, I think that would be something that, ummm…might be a little hard for Santa…"

Sugar Plum tried to save him. "So, Jamal! What OTHER toy would you like?"

"SOCKS!" the mother blurted out.

"NOOO!" screamed Jamal, then turned back to Santa. "A Zombie Hunter Elite Dart Blaster!" More violent head shakes from mom.

Magnus eased Jamal off his lap and shoved him a little too aggressively toward his irate mother. "I promise to bring you a happy surprise, Jamal. You and your mother have a Merry Christmas!"

As his mother dragged him away, Jamal screamed, "Faker! You're a big FAKER!" The other kids in line scrutinized Santa balefully. Magnus looked from them to the folks just beyond the perimeter of SantaVille. Dudley had his arms folded across his chest. He was staring at Magnus, brow furrowed, slowly shaking his head. Right next to Dudley, Cookie and Nick were giving him hopeful smiles they thought were encouraging but felt patronizing: they were the kind they gave every booze-hound loser of a Santa who haunted this wretched place.

Magnus steeled himself. *You are 'Killer' Diller. You've reduced billionaire celebrity CEOs to tears, begging for mercy. Surely you can deal with a bunch of whimpering six-year olds…*

Or maybe not. In quick succession, like a dozen hulking NFL linemen crashing into a hapless tackling dummy, they came at him, one after another, each worse than the last. After it was over, the very worst ones haunted him:

There was the six-year-old Asian-American girl who plopped herself on his lap, stared at him gravely and said (in the manner of Dirty Harry grilling a shifty suspect), "So…if you're the real Santa, what are the names of your reindeer?" When Sugar Plum tried to help him out – "Dasher, Dancer…" – the kid, without taking her eyes of Magnus's face, said "SHUT UP! Santa has to tell me." Magnus's eyes darted up to Dudley. His face was beet-red, and flop sweat was starting to burn his eyes. "Ummmm…oh, wait a minute…Rudolph, right?" And then nothing. The girl just shook her head sadly, removed herself from his lap, and shambled back to her mother. Magnus willed himself not to look at Dudley, but he couldn't help himself. Dudley was wide-eyed in horror. Cookie and Nick were face-palming. It was too much to bear…

Then there was very cute seven-year-old "Mason" – skinny, gentle, dreamy – dressed in a snappy sky-blue blazer and small pink bow tie.

His two dads, both in their mid-50's, both in off-the-rack business casual, were capturing this on their smartphones. The bald skinny one was clicking furiously, while the portly one was pushing the camera toward him, shooting video. When Magnus asked Mason what he wanted for Christmas, the boy said, "I want a Barbie Dream Camper, with Camping Fun Barbie and her two best friends, Midge and Nikki." Magnus was taken aback. "Isn't that something little girls..."

"'SCUSE ME SANTA," said Sugar Plum the Elf. Sugar Plum lifted Mason off Santa's lap, then leaned down and put his arm around his shoulder, palsy-walsy style. "You want a hot tip straight from the toy workshop?" he murmured confidentially. Mason's eyes lit up. Sugar Plum said, "What you REALLY want...is 'Barbie's Dream Private Jet.' Video screen, reclining seats, snack bar with three drink options. 'Nuff said." Mason grinned and gave Sugar Plum a joyous hug, then ran toward his happy parents. The bald one slipped Sugar Plum a fiver as Magnus looked on, baffled.

Every kid who climbed in his lap burst into tears. Every one had a runny nose. Every one wanted some toy Magnus had never heard of, so he had no idea if it was something a parent could buy. With an hour left to go, a determined Hispanic kid named Santiago, nine years old, climbed onto Magnus's lap, unfolded a sheet of notebook paper and said, "Ready?"

Magnus said, "Ummm, I guess so…"

This kid started machine-gunning a list of toys at Magnus that quickly became an incoherent cascade of word salad. "ZipFire Super Soak-Zooka, Elite Delta SlamFire Nerf Blaster, Bullet Barrage Full Clip Action Xtreme First Person Shooter…"

Magnus was dazed by the time the kid looked at him to make sure he got everything. "Ummm, do you have a short list?" said Magnus.

"This IS the short list." Magnus looked up. Dudley was gone, along with Cookie and Nick. Not good. "So," said Santiago, "how about it? You gonna come through for me?"

"Sure, sure, I mean, I'm Santa, right?" The kid smiled and ran back to his mother. Magnus couldn't bear to look at her, after what he'd told her son. He was too exhausted to think about it.

Five minutes until the blessed end of his shift, one more child in line, and Fate or Whatever Mysterious Force Evolved the Universe saved the worst for last. The little girl was about six years old. She was out of control, screaming bloody murder. Her mother was obsessed with putting her on Santa's lap for the family Christmas card photo, but she kept shoving herself off, trying to run away. Of course, the mother blamed Santa for this. "Settle her down, for God's sake! I just want to get a picture. What kind of a Santa Claus ARE you?" Finally Sugar Plum took mercy on him, stuck a candy cane in the girls' mouth, lifted her off

Magnus's lap back into the mall courtyard, and clipped the red velvet rope to the stanchion that shut down SantaVille. Both mother and daughter were screaming as they left: the daughter at mom, the mother at Santa (and by extension the mall). Magnus was dazed. He felt like he'd fallen down an elevator shaft into heavy metal mosh pit, where he'd been pummeled by meth-fueled Satanists. And he hadn't been able to spend a single moment observing life in the mall. A complete bust.

CHAPTER TEN

Magnus, still dressed in his Santa suit, was laid out corpse-still on the lumpy camping cot in the employee break room. The room itself had the austere gloominess of a police holding cell, with a battered avocado green vending machine selling off-brand soft drinks like "Big Fizz Cola," "Dr. Perky" and "Mr. Slurp Root Beer." Magnus didn't care. He had a damp paper towel over his face as the others wandered in for their end-of-day get-together.

Cookie arrived with a platter of oven-fresh white chocolate chunk/Macadamia nut cookies. As weary and wretched as Magnus felt, the smell of those cookies almost caused him to levitate. He was going to sit bolt upright and seize one, but then stopped. *I'm here to spy. Isn't that the whole point of putting myself through this hell?* He dialed into the conversation.

With just the slightest turn of his head, he was able to get his nose to tweak the paper towel so he could see the group with his left eye. He saw an energetic African-American woman in a navy-blue business suit and a copper-skinned man in blue surgical scrubs. A Laurel-and-Hardy skinny and stout pair of 50-something female Bohemians were chatting up a cadaverous older gent in a clerical collar and a jolly geezer in a red-flannel shirt, suspenders and a striped locomotive engineer's hat. "Look," said Cookie, "all I'm saying is that we could do this thing."

"You really think so?" said the African-America woman. (Lawyer?)

"Have you noticed that this place is a total dump?" said the squat boho chick. She picked up a cookie and swallowed it whole. "Nobody wants it. Why would we want to buy it?"

A spike of adrenaline detonated in Magnus's brain. His head jerked up, then slowly descended back on the throw pillow. He didn't see anyone turn toward him. Whew! All at once he was wide-awake and laser focused.

"Because we've put our lives into this dump," said Cookie. Was she the leader of the plot?? "Because we could fix it up to be the place we've always wanted. A kind of, I don't know, 'town center' for the rest of us. Like a community co-op kind of thing."

The gaunt specter of Christian forbearance said, "How pleasant it is when God's people live together in unity! Psalm 133."

The Black lawyer-lady said, "How much do they want?"

Cookie loved that she had a secret worth sharing. "Well, Jazmin – a little bird told me that whoever it is that owns this place…"

Flannel shirt and suspenders said, "Mystery solved. The answer is 'Opportunity Investments,' whatever the hell that is. I'm having a deuce of time getting a handle on them, might be the Mafia. Or maybe CIA…"

Cookie continued. "Well, whoever it is seems to be in a big fat hurry to get rid of it. They're going to unload it for eight hundred thousand, which as far as I can tell is less than the real estate is worth." A cynical chuckle united the group. Cookie was not deterred. "And that same little bird told me they'd take ten percent down just to be rid of it."

Magnus sat up slowly. "Ahhh, excuse me…"

Everyone turned. The pudgy half of Laurel and Hardy said, "Santa! That was some *nice work* out there! Never seen that many kids weeping hysterically. What were you doing, torturing puppies?" Her partner punched her, but with a smile.

Cookie moved toward him in sympathy and handed him a cookie, which he swallowed in two heavenly bites. *OH MY GAWD THESE ARE SO GOOD.* "Roxy!" said Cookie. "He's one of us!

Have some sympathy! I mean, he wouldn't be reduced to doing this if he weren't...I mean, he's obviously had some kind of terrible...I mean..."

Magnus wasn't sure where she was going, but she was rescued by Nick entering with two cardboard trays, four coffees each. "Brain juice, everybody!" He passed out the coffees, handing the last one to Magnus, who slurped it greedily. Nick looked at the table and frowned. "Half a cookie. Thanks everybody.

The skinny half of the Sapphic duo said, "We love you, Nick. We'd do anything for you. You are a kind, generous soul, but you're on your own when it comes to Cookie's baked goods."

"Understood, Louise," he said. "I'd happily do the same to you. Law of the jungle."

The Doctor – Indian? Filipino? Muslim? – said "People, please. Santa has the floor." Once again, everyone turned to him.

"Hello, everyone. I'm Mike, Mike Dillon," said Magnus. "Roxy was right. I had more fun in 'Nam taking Hamburger Hill than I did out there today." *Nice! Playing the 'downtrodden Viet Vet card,* thought Magnus. *You're goooooooood...."*

"You're the fifth Santa we've had this holiday season," said Cookie.

"And the first sober one," said the lawyer.

"I couldn't help overhearing your conversation," said Magnus. *Careful,* he thought. *Easy does it...* "Are you planning on buying this place?"

The Doctor – Magnus could see an emblem on his scrubs that said "Dr. Hakeem" – said, "First, we're going to solve world hunger."

"I thought we were starting with global warming?" said Roxy. "That would take us to 2050."

"Then we'll tackle gun violence," said the Reverend.

"Which takes us till 2080," said Nick. "by which time we'll all be dead."

"By 2080 this place will be worth a hundred dollars, which we'll be able swing even if we ARE dead," said Cookie. Magnus's blink on Cookie was spot-on: a cheerful, determined optimist which, he guessed, was the only way she could survive life in this dump.

"If it's a hundred bucks, we're in," said Roxy, putting her arm around her partner. "Eighty thousand? Not so much."

"Come on, we can do this!" said Cookie. "Do you people *like* paying rent? To be at the mercy of a bunch of faceless, sadistic corporate bullies?"

"Hey!" said Magnus, outraged. Everyone turned to him, surprised. *Whoops. Remember where you are, sport.* "I mean, ummm, hey! Why not? I mean, eight hundred thousand dollars for a shopping mall…"

"An ex-shopping mall," said Roxy. "which is, today, a decrepit pigsty. They should GIVE us this place!"

"The truth!" said the Reverend. "And the truth shall set us free!"

Magnus tried on his best casual, just-one-of-the-peasants voice. "So," he said, "where you'd hear about this fire sale?"

Nick laughed. "Why? Are you thinking of out-bidding us?" Everyone chuckled at this.

Lanky Louise said to the group, "Hey, he's Santa! He knows people! Toymakers, retailers…I bet he knows Jeff Bezos personally!" She turned to Magnus. "Do you?"

Magnus did know Jeff Bezos, but he snorted derisively. "Nope. And no, I'm currently trying to raise the funds for a McDonalds 'value meal.' So I'm not your competition."

Roxy turned to Cookie. "Soooo…who is your little bird?"

Cookie looked at flannel shirt and suspenders. "Archie."

Archie was brushing the cookie crumbs out of his beard when he heard his name. He revealed his confidence. "Got a man on the inside."

Magnus's eyes widened for a single moment, then re-set. Archie said, "Old pal from law school, swore me to secrecy, that's all I can say. You want more, you'll have to beat it out of me…or give me another cookie."

Magnus stared at him. *Fletcher? Hard to believe. Then again, they're about the same age…*

Cookie brought the group back to her passion project. "Eighty thousand is nothing!"

"For THIS group?" said Roxy, then grimaced.

"Okay, it's not nothing, but it's…I mean, let's dream a little. Just see where we are. The goal is eighty thousand dollars. Who'd be willing to pony up what?"

A long pause. Everyone looked at each other. Nick finally broke the silence. "I have a whole-life insurance policy. I think I can borrow against it."

"How much?" said Cookie.

"Mmmm…maybe twenty thousand dollars."

"Twenty thousand dollars!" said Cookie. "We're halfway to being halfway there! So, who else?"

Archie said, "I got some junk-silver survival coins."

"Survival coins?" said Jazmin.

"Yeah. I went through a period when…I had a kind of…"

"Nervous breakdown," said the Reverend. "Like I did."

"Yeah, very similar. Right after 9/11. Law firm got rid of me, so did the wife…except unlike the Rev, I kind of went down kind of a rabbit hole. I got into some serious survivalist shit. I was…oh, what's the word?"

"Crazy?" said Roxy.

"Yeah, that's word I was looking for. I went all-in: bought five years' worth of freeze-dried ice cream, learned to use a bow-and-arrow, make jerky out of deer meat. And bought some survival coins."

"Why are they called 'survival coins?'" asked Jazmin.

"Well, during the zombie apocalypse, the money itself won't be worth shit, but the SILVER in the coins…" He tapped his head. "I almost bought a time-share in an abandoned missile silo."

"So how much are the coins worth?" said Cookie.

"I'm guessing about ten, fifteen thousand."

"Thirty-five thousand!" raved Cookie. "Okay, so who else?"

"Well…" said Dr. Hakeem. "I don't have any cash, or an insurance policy…" Everyone was looking at him with hopeful faces. "But, well, I have two functioning kidneys. And I know for a fact I could get twenty-six thousand dollars on the black market…"

A collective groan went up from the group. "Thanks," said Cookie, "but no thanks. We draw the line at harvesting organs."

"I'd be willing to sell my Prius," said lithe Louise. "It's a 2014, has about eighty thousand miles. Should be worth, I'm thinking, maybe nine thousand dollars…"

"Do what you want, but don't expect to borrow my F-150," said Roxy.

Louise threw her hands up in dismay, then pointed at her partner. "My partner of fourteen years, everyone!"

"You'll always have my love," said Roxy, "but you'll never have my car keys."

"Forty-four thousand!" said Cookie. "Who else? C'mon people…"

"I have but one vestige of my previous life," said the Reverend. "The McMansion in North Dallas, that's gone, along with the condo on Kaanapali Beach in Maui. And my sweet Mercedes convertible is gone…" With this, the Rev seemed to drift off into a reverie. "S63 Cabriolet. 577 horsepower, zero to sixty in four seconds. Only 130 of them ever built, and I had one." Magnus couldn't help staring. *Previous life? Who was this guy? He must have been loaded. What happened?*

"And of course the Gulfstream G650.." Magnus jumped as if he'd been tasered. *This skinny sonofabitch had a better jet than I have.* He went on. "I had to lose everything to regain my soul. The one relic from the past is this." He produced a gold cigarette lighter. "My eighteen-karat solid gold Zippo lighter. I used it to smoke crystal meth when I went on the down-low in Boys Town, which is, of course, how I got caught, thank God, pun intended. I've kept it all these years to remind myself of who I was, how far I fell, and how far I've come. But...well, I'm not sure I need it anymore. Cost me fifteen thousand new, and I bet we can get twelve thousand on eBay."

Magnus had to force himself to stop staring, because everyone else seemed to know all this about the Rev. "So, let's say twelve thousand," said Cookie. "That puts us at fifty-six thousand dollars! And I can make up the rest if I sell the recipe for my chocolate chip..."

"NOOO!" shouted the group in unison, jolting Magnus. "You are NOT going to make somebody a hundred million dollars," said Nick, "by selling the recipe for the best chocolate chip cookies on earth! No no no no NO!"

"But look, it's for something I really want..."

"Over my dead body," said Nick. He looked around. "Anybody else want in on this? Dead bodies?" Everyone raised their hands, including Magnus. "That's settled!" Cookie shook her head in frustration even as she smiled in gratitude. Magnus felt something in the room, something unfamiliar. A feeling. Was it...love? These people really loved each other.

He was just relaxing into that feeling when Dudley stuck his head in the door. "Santa? My office, now," and then disappeared. Everyone looked at Magnus apprehensively as he stood and shuffled to the door.

"Good luck!" said Cookie. Magnus nodded, and lingered for a single second. "That was one incredible cookie," he said, then strode off to the guillotine that awaited.

CHAPTER ELEVEN

Dudley plopped himself behind his desk. The furrowed brow, the darting eyes, the vein throbbing in his forehead: he was agitated and struggling to maintain his executive command posture. He motioned for Magnus to take a seat as he opened a bottom drawer, chunked out four Ibuprofen, and dry swallowed them. "Sooooooo…how'd your first day go?"

Magnus was startled by this. Dudley had seen how it had gone, he was there for the first (and worst) twenty minutes. What was he supposed to say? "It was…ummm…challenging."

Dudley lurched back, incredulous. "Challenging? CHALLENGING? It was TERRIFYING! It was the Hindenburg crashing into the Word Trade Center! Even the drunk Santas were better than you! Can we just take a moment so I can share some of these feedback cards?"

"That's not really…" but there was no stopping Dudley. He picked up a small stack of brick red three-by five cards, shuffling through them for the "best" feedback.

"Let's start with the gentler ones. 'Worst Santa ever.'" He flicked to another. "Our Dentist is less scary than this jerk." Another. "My child can't stop crying." Another. "I've been coming here for fourteen years, the last six just for the cookies, but never, ever again after what happened.'" Dudley looked up at Magnus.

"You just can't please some people.…"

Dudley threw the stack of cards at him. They hit him in the face then fluttered to the floor. He reached inside his desk, popped a square of "Kwit-O-Rette" nicotine gum, and started chewing furiously. "Some people?!? I saw you out there, it was…oh, what's the right word? Gruesome? Hideous? Tragic? It was like they hated you on sight, every single one of them! You have a kind of genius gift for terrifying kids. I'm dying of curiosity. What possible reason would you have for wanting to be a shopping mall Santa?"

Magnus said, "Well, I…"

Dudley cut him off. "Doesn't make a goddamn bit of difference." He reached into a side drawer, squirted hand sanitizer and friction-washed his hands. "You, my friend, are fired. Pick up your shit and get out." He handed him an envelope. "One day's pay. Enough for a bender and a cheap hotel room to sleep it off. Goodbye."

Magnus panicked. *This wrecks everything.* He opened his mouth to beg for another chance when Cookie and Nick flung open the door and barged in. Nick said, "I hope you haven't…"

"I have," said Dudley, cutting him off. "You're too late."

"We think you should give Mike another chance," said Cookie. Magnus was shocked. *What's this about? Who am I to her?*

"Really?" said Dudley, clearly astonished. "Why?"

Nick said, "Okay, he's had a bit of a rough start.…"

"A…bit…of…a…rough…start?" said Dudley, enunciating each word. "This mall has nine loyal customers and he's chased off fourteen of them!"

"…but Cookie and I think we can help him."

There was a brief stare down. Then Cookie said, "Do you have another Santa lined up?"

This stopped Dudley. "Well…no. But burning down SantaVille would generate more goodwill for this place than soldiering on with Krampus the Christmas Devil here."

"Dudley," said Cookie in a soft, soothing voice. "It's that time of year, when we stop thinking about ourselves and start thinking of others. Open your heart. He's our Tiny Tim, all alone in the world. Don't be a Scrooge."

Magnus shot a pathetic look at Dudley, who looked away and folded his arms across his chest. Cookie said, "Give us one day to coach him. One day. C'mon, be a hero."

After a long moment, Dudley sighed deeply, opened another desk drawer, took out an asthma inhaler and atomized himself. Finally he relented. "One day, and that's it." Cookie and Nick smiled. Magnus did too, but for a different reason. *With any luck, I'll only need one more day…*

CHAPTER TWELVE

Cookie had offered Magnus a home-cooked meal, and he eagerly accepted. She lived on the third floor: unit three eighteen of a weary cell-block apartment building plopped in a huddle of similar tumbledowns, all hastily assembled from inter-changeable parts in the early 1950s. They were built to last twenty years. Seventy years later they reminded Magnus of the forlorn codgers panhan-dling with hand-drawn cardboard signs at freeway offramps: exhausted, decrepit and desper-ate.

Inside? That was a different story. He was sur-prised. The place was a festival of budget Christmas cheer, anchored by a too-tall Christmas tree bumping into the cottage-cheese ceiling. The tree was groaning with a bazillion homemade or-naments and thousands of multi-colored blinking lights. Over-sized red and white paper "snow-flakes" hung from the ceiling, illuminated by fifty mason jar candles. All the framed artwork in the house – and there was a lot – was covered by jolly wrapping paper, with huge festive bows. A garland made of olive branches and holly graced the mantel.

Magnus was just finishing the meal that Cookie had fixed for him. He subscribed to Bon Appetit magazine, and regularly directed his personal chef to prepare cutting-edge dishes ("Braised Ox-Tails With Vietnamese Sizzling Rice Crepes") from the trendiest restaurants in Manhattan. He'd completely forgotten just how delectable really *great* meatloaf was. *Man, this stuff is delicious! Slow down, I can't stop shoveling this into my face…* The rest of the plate was just as good: a (light!) potato salad made with Yukon Golds, asparagus and olives, and a savory stovetop hash that combined Brussels sprouts, crispy sage and walnuts. The good news is that Cookie assumed that "Mike" hadn't had a decent meal in twenty years, so she smiled as he wolfed the platter of food she'd set before him. "Oh, man, this is wonderful!" gushed Magnus. "You've got the gift! Thank you so much!"

"My pleasure," she said.

"And those cookies! Where'd you learn to do all this?" said Magnus.

Cookie looked off into the distance, conjuring a memory. "I had kind of a rough childhood, ran away from home when I was fourteen. This couple rescued me, literally took me off the street and put me to work in their bakery. Oscar and Sadie Schumann, Schumann's Bakery. Sadie showed me how to do everything: cheesecakes, mousse cakes, breads, tarts, Italian donuts, bread pudding, salted caramel brownies…I can still make a mean Swedish Princess Cake. And, of course, cookies. I loved baking cookies because they made everyone so happy, especially little kids. And ever since then…I don't know, it's just what I love to do. And I love that people love what I do. What more could you want from life?"

This hit Magnus like a fist to the nose. *Making cookies is the secret to life?* But here she was, an authentically happy woman. Content in a way that Magnus had never been his whole life. He'd spent his life lusting after the one thing he could never, ever have: MORE. So who was the genius here?

"That story may have sounded kind of sad, but it's not. I'm having a delightful life," said Cookie.

"Then why aren't you rich? I mean, those cookies…"

Cookie laughed. "Okay, there is one other sad thing that happened to me…" She paused, collecting herself. "I got married too young to the wrong man. He was the Schumann's son: a handsome, charming, feckless abusive alcoholic. I did the stupidest thing imaginable: I made it my life's work to show him how my love could save him from himself. Of course, the harder I tried, the angrier he got. He finally put me in the hospital with a broken jaw. I decided to get out, and all I had was a gray metal box of three by five cards with my recipes: everything Sadie had taught me about baking. Nick – I mean Coffee Nick at the mall, he's a magnificent guy, I wish I'd met him thirty years ago – he gave me a free cup of coffee when I told him what I wanted to do. I baked him a sheet of chocolate chip cookies, and he gave up half his space so I could open Cookie's Cookies. Pretty soon I had my own space, and…well, here I am. And there's not a day I don't get down on my knees and thank God for the good fortune to be single, debt-free, and doing what I love."

"I'd like to be debt-free too, Cookie. Can I pay you back for this magnificent dinner?"

"No need," she said.

"I don't mean money out of my pocket, since I'm busted. I want to give you something better. I want to make you filthy rich." She burst out laughing. "No, seriously! Your cookies are…they're the best! Better than the best, they're unique! I've never had a cookie where I could I could taste every single ingredient: the chocolate, the vanilla, the brown sugar, even the salt! Crisp on the outside, chewy on the inside. This isn't a cookie, it's a dream of a cookie."

She started to make coffee. "Okay, I'm listening. What's this plan of yours?"

"Okay, first we're going to patent your recipe and trademark the name 'Cookie's Cookies,' if its available."

"When you say 'we'…"

"I mean, you know, 'us,' in the mall," said Magnus. "We can get, oh, what's her name, Jazmin, to help with the legal stuff. If not her, we'll find someone else."

"We will?" said Cookie, looking bemused. "And then what? Who's going to make the cookies, sell them, all that?"

"No, no," said Magnus. "See, this is why you need me. You have to make a plan, think strategically. After we've covered ourselves legally…" Magnus lowered his voice, letting Cookie in on the secret. "Then we find the hippest bistro in Manhattan, with a big-deal celebrity chef, the bigger the better. You bake him some cookies. He tastes one, has an orgasm, and then we make him an offer he can't refuse."

"Which is?" said Cookie.

"Easy. We offer him an exclusive: he and he alone gets to feature your cookies on his dessert menu. We tip a couple of big-noise food critics about the hottest new dessert in New York. They naturally go wild, and then their readers go wild. Twitter goes wild. Facebook goes wild. And suddenly YOU, Cookie…is that your real name, by the way?"

"My real name is Alice Ballenger," she said, pouring two cups of coffee.

Magnus launched back into his spiel. Gawd, he was good at this! "And suddenly YOU, Alice Ballenger, known to the world as 'Cookie' of 'Cookie's Cookies' are red-hot. Everybody in America, in the WORLD wants this legendary cookie. Sooo…" smiled Magnus, "What's our next move?"

"Beats me," said Cookie, sipping her coffee. "We, ummm, sell the recipe for a million dollars?"

Magnus scoffed. "Bigger, Cookie, think BIGGER! We build ten thousand pop-up cookie kitchens all across America – malls, urban centers, theme parks, sports and concert venues – offering Cookie's Cookies for one month only. ONE MONTH! And then, who knows, they might be gone forever!" He paused, sipped his coffee. She was staring at him. *I've got her!* "And here's the genius part: we make sure that each pop-up has a limited amount of cookie batter, so it's guaranteed to run out when the lines are the longest."

Cookie was taken aback. "Why would we…"

"The buzz, Cookie! Social media! People want what they can't have. When word gets out there's a shortage of Cookie's Cookies…well, imagine the viral videos of two-hour lines in Times Square to get one of your amazing cookies. And THAT'S when we shut EVERYTHING down! That's when we release our IPO, sit back and let the billionaires beat the shit out of each other to see which one can hand us the biggest, most ridiculous check to capitalize Cookie's Cookies."

Cookie's mouth was open. Magnus could tell she was boggled by his genius. Finally she said, "Then what?"

"Then it's whatever you want, Cookie. Two thousand mall stores? Supermarket point of purchase? Online and catalog mail order? Licensing agreements with Starbucks? Cookbooks? Your own show on the Food Channel? It's all yours, you earned it. And one thing is absolutely certain."

"What's that?" she said, a bit dazed.

"When it's all over, you and your friends can *buy* the Paradise Valley Shopping Plaza." Magnus was expecting her to burst into tears, throw her arms around him and thank him for illuminating the path to a billion-dollar cookie empire. Instead, she burst out laughing. She laughed so hard she snorted coffee through her nose, which made her laugh even harder. "What?" said Magnus, baffled.

"Oh Mike, you're a caution! That was the wildest thing I've ever heard!" The laugh finally wound down to a burping giggle as Cookie sipped her coffee.

"We can do this, Cookie. Really." And then Magnus saw the way she was looking at him. With pity. "Look, I've had some hard luck, but…but I used to be…"

"Used to be what?" she said.

He gulped. What could he tell her that she would believe? "You may find this hard to believe, but I actually know people who…"

Cookie laughed again, more gently this time, as she reached out and put her hand on his. "I'm sure you do, Mike, and I appreciate your wanting to help me. It's fun to dream, isn't it? But the world is…"

"Tough," he said. He sipped his coffee.

Cookie looked into her cup. "It took me five years of working my tail off every day in Nick's coffee stall to scrape together the money to open up my own little store in this crappy little mall. I've got my customers, my friends, and so many beautiful children. Every day I give people this tiny little moment of perfect happiness. I love that."

Magnus nodded. "Uh huh."

"I don't want to own the Paradise Valley Shopping Plaza. That would make me miserable. I just want to bake and sell my cookies. And speaking of cookies…" She got up and moved back into the kitchen.

As he watched her take the pan out of the oven, Magnus knew he'd made a mistake. As he watched Cookie bustle about her kitchen, he felt something odd. What was it? It took him a moment, and then he knew: it was that feeling again, the one he had with Stacy, eating potato salad and listening to Dixieland jazz. Only this time he knew he wasn't being bamboozled. Cookie was so different from the other women he'd met. Honest, earthy, straight-forward. A good heart. Happy. She smiled as she plopped a plate of cookies in front of him. "Ever had a 'brookie'? Half cookie, half brownie." Magnus was still glassy-eyed, pondering his revelation as he picked one up and bit into it. Oh man. Chocolate chip cookie on top, fudge brownie on the bottom. Magnus felt like weeping. Why wasn't there a statue to this woman in every town square in America? How often do you experience perfection? It was today's "Best Thing He'd Ever Tasted."

"Well?" said Cookie.

"I keep thinking that whatever the last kind of cookie you give me is the absolute best ever created. And then you give me something like this. I'm…thunderstruck. Flabbergasted. Stupefied."

They sat there together, eating brookies and sipping coffee, Magnus reverting back to his childhood habit of trying to take the smallest bites he could to make it last as long as possible. As he vacuumed up the last bite, licking each finger one by one and chasing the sugar rush with a swig of java, he remembered his mission. "You know," he said, "I really admire your plan to buy the mall. Very ambitious."

"Thanks," she said. "We're not quite there yet, but, well…"

Magnus knew he had to keep this casual. "Tell me, how'd you drive down the price? I bet that took some diabolical planning."

Cookie looked at him like he'd lost his mind. "Planning? Archie told me about that deal two days ago."

"Archie?" said Magnus.

"Yeah, you know, Archie. Gramps. Guy who runs the toy store."

Magnus was baffled. "Well, how'd you get all the anchor stores to bail?"

Cookie gave out a righteous hoot of laughter. "Oh, that! That was easy. First, we had the mall cut way back on maintenance and security, so the whole place became dirty and dangerous. And then we arranged for a big, new, sexy, clean, safe, super-fun mall to be built just seven miles away!"

Magnus felt the bottom fall out of his stomach. There was no possible way he could be wrong about everything…could he? He flashed on what this meant, the deal he'd made with the Brain Trust. He was going to lose the bet, and he was going to lose it in a way that would ruin his business. They'd stop being afraid of him. He'd have to fire them and start over. Dwayne too? He wasn't done shaping Dwayne, although winning this bet might be his graduation present…

A knock at the door. Cookie got up to answer. She came back with Nick and a skinny Hispanic kid in a heavy metal hoody and torn jeans.

Something about this kid seemed familiar. Cookie vanished into the kitchen as Nick did the honors. "Mike? This is Diego. We understand this is Meat Loaf Nite at Cookie's Kitchen. Diego, this is Mike. He's our resident Santa Claus." Diego sat down next to Magnus, with Nick across from him.

"Hiya," said Diego, staring at the brookies. Nick nodded and Diego powered one down in two bites. That's when the light bulb went on for Magnus. *The homeless kid who thinks he lives here.* His eyes went wide as he glanced at Nick, who read him perfectly.

"I'm sure Dudley mentioned the menace of the mall, right? The homeless kid who lives with us? The one no one can catch?"

"Yeah," said Magnus. "He showed me a blurry picture on his cellphone. Is this..." Cookie appeared with two heaping plates of food. Magnus was full, but his mouth still watered as he eyeballed Diego's plate. Then Nick, Diego and Cookie all bowed their heads.

Nick did the honors. "Dear Lord, dear God, dear Heavenly Oneness, thank you for the infinite blessings of our wonderful lives. Bless this food so it will give us the strength to do Your work in the world. A very humble and grateful Amen."

Only then did they dive in. Nick's words echoed in Magnus's mind. *Infinite blessings of our wonderful lives. That's how they think of themselves.* He could tell they believed it a hundred percent.

Nick broke this reverie with a nod toward Diego. "We found him sleeping on one of the beds in that mattress store that went belly up."

"Poor thing," said Cookie. "Hadn't eaten in five days."

"She gave me a cookie," said Diego.

"Well…seven cookies," said Cookie. "He inhaled them."

"Did something happen to your folks?" said Magnus.

"Yeah," said Diego, biting into the second slab of meat loaf. "They found out I'm gay. My dad beat the crap out of me and tossed me out of the house."

"That was six months ago," said Nick. "Dudley's been on the warpath the whole time."

"And Mall Security hasn't been able to catch him?"

Cookie looked at Nick, who looked at Magnus. "Mike, have you noticed that we don't have any Mall Security officers?"

"Budget cuts," said Cookie. "Dudley told us to put the local cops on speed dial, that would take care of everything."

"Yeah," said Nick, "except for all the kids who hang around and steal us blind." Nick noticed Magnus staring at Diego. "He's not one of them, Mike."

"He's one of us," said Cookie.

"I hired Diego to do some stuff around the shop," said Nick. "Sweep, re-stock cream and sugar, stuff like that. One day he started messing around with my computer. Turns out the kid is a genius. Now he works for everyone: does the ordering, does the books…he started a rewards system that pings my best customers with free offers, stuff like that."

"And all we have to do is slip him food and hide him when Dudley snoops around," said Cookie.

"We're getting the best of that deal," said Nick. Diego looked up at the coffee king, who smiled. "Oh, did I say that out loud? Dang, stupid me." The both laughed. Nick turned to Magnus. "So don't even think about ratting him out to Dudley, unless you want us to un-save your job."

Magnus had been considering that. "Okay, okay, I get it."

"Now, let's talk about tomorrow," said Nick. "And how we're going to save your job. I hope there's plenty of coffee, because we've got a *lot* of work to do."

CHAPTER THIRTEEN

A gimlet-eyed Dudley watched as Magnus, Nick, Cookie and Archie approached "SantaVille." Sugar Plum the Elf was chatting up the short line of kids waiting to see Santa. He did a discreet double-take at Santa's new helpers. Nick was now Sugar Plum's (very) big brother elf, authentic down to his green and red elf boots with metallic gold pom poms. Cookie was dolled up as Mrs. Claus: a red velour dress with white faux fur trim, black belt with a gold buckle and a matching Santa hat.

Nick was carrying a large tray of mini-coffee cups, which the parents in line eagerly plucked up. Cookie carried a spacious, beribboned basket filled with individually wrapped chocolate chip cookies. As Nick and Cookie stationed themselves on either side of Santa's throne, Archie handed Sugar Plum a bag of small toys, plush animals and stocking stuffer novelties. The elf smiled, gave Archie a single nod, and placed the bag on the ground within grabbing distance.

The day hadn't started yet, but Magnus was sweating. It wasn't just the costume: it was the crash course he'd undergone last night: How To Be Jolly. It hadn't been easy. Magnus prided himself on being a quick study, but learning to be good-natured? Warm? Sensitive to the needs of others? Magnus had six decades of life to unlearn. First they had to teach him to RELAX. Then they had to show him how to get out of his own monkey-brain, read the kids' body language and listen to what they said . *You're there to comfort these kids,* Cookie said. *You're there to serve them. To love them.* LOVE these nasty, sweaty little crumb-crushers? WHY? HOW??

Magnus couldn't seem to master it, but Cookie and Nick wouldn't give up. Three hours in, they turned from coaching him to drilling him, with Diego playing the part of a bratty kid. He used the words they gave him and repeated their instructions. RELAX. LISTEN. LOVE. Gradually he got better, until, as midnight approached, he seemed to be as good as he was going to get, which was almost good enough. A series of questions lingered in the back of Magnus's mind: *why are they doing this? What's in it for them? Why do they care? Could they possibly know who I really am? If so, how?*

But help him they did, and now it was *show-time*. Sugar Plum whispered, "You ready to light this candle?" Magnus nodded. *Relax Listen Love Relax Listen Love Relax Listen Love. Okay, let's do this thing.* Sugar Plum rolled the "Santa Will Be Back Shortly" sign out of the way, unsnapped the red velour rope and the line surged forward.

First in line was a cherubic six-year-old African American girl. She rushed up to him and clambered onto his lap. Magnus could see Cookie chatting up the girl's mother as they both sipped Nick's coffee. The girl looked right into Santa's eyes.

"Uhhh, welcome! To the North Pole! And what is your name…" Magnus was cut off by Cookie.

"Oh, Santa, what a kidder! You know very well who this is! This is your friend Diamond!"

"Diamond!' said Sugar Plum. "What a lovely name!"

"Diamond!" said Magnus. "Silly me, of course! How could I forget a name like that! Ho ho ho!" Nick had coached Magnus for a full forty-five minutes on how to deliver a properly hearty, full bellied "ho ho ho." Magnus stole a quick glance at Dudley, who was taken aback. Good!

"Oh, Santa, here's that extra-special cookie you asked me to make for Diamond!" Cookie leaned down and give Diamond the cookie, and then stepped back.

"Of course!" Diamond was looking at Magnus with ecstatic amazement, and with that look all his anxious fear drained away, leaving only a glow of wonder. This little girl adored him! "And what would you..."

"Santa!" He looked up at Cookie. She was palming a flash card with a picture of a bicycle on it, aimed so the parents couldn't see. She was smiling and nodding. It took him a moment, but then he remembered the training...

"I know what you'd like for Christmas, Diamond!"

"You do?"

"A bicycle! Am I right?" With that, Diamond stood on the seat of the throne and threw her arms around Santa's neck. Magnus was so surprised he barely noticed her shoes kicking his groin. He looked up and saw Diamond's mother, glowing with delight...and also saw Dudley, utterly baffled by this radical 180 in Magnus's demeanor. Magnus said, "Diamond, the elves have been working overtime to make sure you get just the kind of bike you want!"

"Thank you, Santa, oh THANK YOU!" she said. Then Cookie handed her a small toy giraffe and everyone huddled together as Sugar Plum walked the mother into SantaVille, plopped her next to Santa, took her smartphone and tapped off a series of commemorative photos. For a man who had spent his entire life avoiding photographers, Magnus was surprised how much he enjoyed this.

CHAPTER FOURTEEN

This was something new for Magnus. He'd spent his whole life as Alpha Male One, the Big Noise, the Prime Mover. Now here he was, just part of this beautiful machine that produced happy kids and delighted parents. Actually it was worse than that: he was the weak link. These people around him, they were carrying him. The machine was designed to conceal his inexperience and empathy deficit. He felt like the no-talent star of a Broadway musical, but it didn't make a bit of difference because everyone around him sang and danced and made him look like he belonged there.

The children in line watched the ones before them, so they were ready for Santa to be a jolly psychic. All Magnus had to do was bounce the kid on his knee, wait for Cookie to feed him the kid's name and show him the flashcard of what she'd gleaned from the parent. Santa got his big moment: a dollhouse! Hot Wheels! Headphones! Chutes and Ladders! He was surprised that such simple things could make these kids so happy. Then came the cookie – how they loved that cookie! – and then the photo. After an hour of non-stop Santa stardom, Dudley threw his hands up and went back to scouring the mall for Diego. Things were working so well that Magnus started to relax…until Camila sat on his lap.

Camila was a melancholy five-year-old Hispanic girl. When Magnus looked at Cookie for a cue about her Christmas wish, Cookie shrugged. She was standing next to Camila's father, a stooped man with a weathered face and a gloomy demeanor who also shrugged his shoulders: he had no clue what his daughter wanted. Magnus knew he was going to have to work for this one. "So, Camila! Welcome to the North Pole! What would you like Santa to bring you for Christmas?"

Camila looked up at Magnus with soulful brown eyes and said, "I want my mommy to come back." Magnus felt like somebody had stuck a dagger in his chest. His eyes shot up to the girl's father, who was shocked as well.

"Camila!" he said. "You know Mommy has gone to heaven. You *promised* me that if I let you see Santa, you wouldn't…"

Before he could finish, Cookie had taken Camila from Santa's lap and wrapped her in a loving mama bear hug. "Oh, Camila," she said, "Santa and I have been waiting for you all day!"

"You have?" she said.

"We have?" said Magnus. "Err, I mean, right! We have!"

Cookie was rocking the girl gently, stroking her ebony hair. "Your mother in heaven told us what a good, brave, helpful girl you've been all year, and she loves you soooooo much she had Santa's elves make you something very special." Magnus saw Nick grab a rainbow-colored stuffed animal with gold dragon wings and put it in Cookie's hand. "This is Angel Kitty. This is so you'll know that your mommy in heaven is watching over you every minute of every day." Camila's eyes went wide. She squeezed the angel kitty, then plunged back into Cookie's arms, sobbing with joy.

There was nothing for Magnus to do but sit there and observe this tiny miracle. His eyes went from Camila to Cookie, who was crying as well. Magnus couldn't help himself: his eyes started to mist up. He was feeling something he'd never felt before. What was it? It wasn't that lovey-dovey feeling he'd had earlier. It was…awe. He was in the presence of someone who really knew how to love and care for others, by instinct.

He'd spent his entire life in a kind of cynical trance, explaining his own zero-sum attitude by refusing to believe there was any other way forward in this fallen world. He remembered – was it really just last week? – that he'd told Dwayne there was no such thing as love, that life was nothing but a never-ending round of 'Let's Make a Deal.' Lord Almighty, how wrong he'd been. And he'd never been so happy to be wrong in his entire life.

CHAPTER FIFTEEN

Almost done! Just one more mommy-daughter pair in line, and then Magnus could luxuriate in one of Cookie's ethereal cookies – Snickerdoodles today, fat and chewy, yum yum – chased with a cup of Nick's fierce espresso roast java. A buoyant dark-skinned woman in her early twenties, with jet black hair flowing from a center part, was holding her eager four-year-old daughter by the hand. The girl was resplendent in a Frida Kahlo-inspired party dress: a riot of stylized red, pink and magenta flower blooms on black velvet, with lace trim. She had a large red gardenia in her hair. Cookie was chatting up mom as the daughter raced up to Magnus and climbed into his lap. "Say hello to Sofia!" said Cookie.

"Well, Sofia, welcome to SantaVille!" said Magnus. He was relaxed now, confident and in control.

"What a wonderful dress! Looks like you fell down in the world's most beautiful flower patch!" She giggled. "So what would you like Santa to bring you for Christmas? No, don't tell me!" He glanced up at Cookie, who flicked up a flash card Magnus had seen before. "I bet you'd like…I know…a great big Crayola Coloring set, with crayons, markers, construction paper…"

"BITCH!" The word exploded the air like a shrapnel grenade. From out of nowhere, three heavily tatted men in white t-shirts and chinos appeared. The biggest of the three grabbed the woman and wrenched her arm back. "She's my daughter, bitch. You've been hiding her, and I'm here to take her!"

"Get away from me!" The woman jerked her arm away and pulled back. Her black eyes blazed with hatred. "The Judge told you to stay the hell away from us!"

The well-muscled young man was having none of this. "I don't give a shit what that Judge said, she ain't here right now, and Sofia is MINE!"

Nick tried to move between them. "Look, pal, let's just settle down and…" The man punched Nick in the stomach. Then the man shoved the woman out of the way, turned, and started for the girl. Magnus could feel her trembling in his lap. From out of nowhere, Cookie grabbed his right wrist and pushed his left shoulder with the butt of her hand, and he fell backwards across her outstretched left leg. *Cookie knows Aikido?* She had her knee on his chest and started punching him in the face.

Elapsed time since this fracas began: eight seconds.

The man's cohorts leapt in, shoving Cookie off their friend. One of them pinned her and was about to give her face a backhand slap when Magnus amazed himself. He moved the girl off his lap and dove from Santa's throne, bashing into Cookie's assailant like an NFL linebacker and knocking him off her. And then – how did this happen? – all three of the men were on Magnus! Holy crap! One held him down. One slugged him in the stomach. The biggest one, the boyfriend, hunkered down on his knees, reared back and delivered a lights-out fist to his face. The last thing Magnus remembered before everything went black was the faint, strangled voice of that poor little girl sobbing. "They've killed him, Mommy! They've killed Santa! What's going to happen to Christmas?"

CHAPTER SIXTEEN

Blackness. A void. No sound, no light. *I smell something! Acrid, corrosive, like bleach. And wait a minute…what's that? Far off, ten miles away, but…something. Isn't that…a baby crying? And moaning of some sort. And…hold on…Nick's voice!*

"The man is injured. Take a look at him, some really bad folks beat the crap out of him, he may have brain damage. He needs to be looked at right now."

A woman. Who is this? "First things first, Sir. Give me his insurance information so we can admit him and have a look."

"Here's his wallet, his I.D. and his Medicare card."

"Okay, let me quickly run these. Stay right there."

Another voice. That Doctor, the swarthy guy in the break room. Is he here too, wherever this is?

"Excuse me, my name is Doctor Hakeem Noorani, I'm a friend. I can certify that this man's injuries warrant immediate medical attention."

"Do you have admitting privileges at this hospital, Dr. Noorani?"

"Well, no, but…"

"Do you know a doctor here who has admitting privileges?"

"No, I don't."

"Then you'll have to wait while we make sure we can admit him."

Hey, I've got insurance! Hello! Why can't you hear me?

"Good thing he has Medicare…"

Cookie's voice! Cookie is here too?? Cookie, it's me, Mike!

"I'm sorry, this Medicare card is a fake."

What??

"We get a lot of these. And his driver's license is also a fake…"

I have a gold-plated health insurance plan, a freakin' PPO, dammit! I can pay for this! I can probably buy this damn hospital and fire your asses!

"I'm very sorry, but there's nothing I can do…"

There IS something you can do! You can keep me from dying!

"Is there anyone else we can talk to?"

"I'm afraid not. Not unless you can prove who he is and prove to us that he has insurance."

I'm MAGNUS DILLER!! Call Dwayne, he knows who I am! Or Fletcher!

"Okay. Thanks."

Oh God, what's going on? Why can't anyone hear me? Why can't I see anything? What's happening to me?

"What now? Anywhere else we can try?"

Nick, can you hear me?

"The nearest public hospital is two hours away. I'm sure they'll turn us away if we don't find Mike's real I.D."

Dr. Hakeem, listen to me, I can explain everything…

"I think we ought to take him back to my place, let Dr. Hakeem do what he can and then let him rest."

Cookie. Don't let me die, Cookie. Oh, please, please…

"Yeah, okay. Let's go."

Don't let me die like this. How did I get here? What's happening to me? I don't want to die. Don't let me die.

The sound faded out. Silence. Blackness. Nothing. And then, something! What was it? *Cookie's face! He could see Cookie's face from earlier that day, looking at that poor girl who wanted her mother back. Cookie's beautiful, radiant face, there to love that little girl. Love, perfect love, nothing but love.* Magnus held onto that luminous, loving face as long as he could, until it faded to nothing.

An eternity of nothing.

A void.

Death.

CHAPTER SEVENTEEN

"Coffee here, and some fresh cookies. I'll put another washcloth on his forehead."

That's Cookie's voice! I can hear her! I'm alive! Oh god oh god oh god! Christmas carols on the radio! Silent Night! And that smell! Oh my god, cookies! Chocolate chip cookies! I must be in Cookie's apartment!

"Is he out of danger, Doc?" *That's Nick.*

"Hard to say." *Dr. Hakeem is here! Why?* "Best case, it's just a broken nose and a bad concussion and he'll find his way back to us." *That's good! Yes!* "Worst case, well..." *What? WHAT??* "That guy really punched his lights out. Might be some permanent brain damage, or...or worse." *What can be worse than that? Oh no. NO....*

Magnus could feel himself being probed: A cold metal device poking his ears, thumb and index finger opening his eyes. *I'm here! I'M HERE!!*

Magnus was screaming, but the sounds weren't traveling from his brain to his vocal cords.

"He belongs in a hospital." *Dr. Hakeem. No shit, Sherlock.*

"Weird about the fake I.D. Why would a guy like this have fake I.D.? I mean, who is this guy? *I'm Magnus "Killer" Diller, Nick! I'm somebody! Somebody BIG!*

Doorbell. Door open and close. Voices. *The Reverend? And that kid, what's his name…Diego. Kid goes right for the cookies, I can hear him chewing.*

"So, how'd it go?" *says Nick. How did what go?*

"Goodwill comes to those who are generous and lend freely, who conduct their affairs with justice." *What is the Reverend talking about?*

"That's terrific, Rev, but what does that mean in dollars and cents?"

"Roxy and Louise generously contributed two hundred dollars they had reserved for the purchase of gifts for one another. Archie handed me fifty dollars right out of his register. And that African American gentleman in your coffee shop, Nick? Darnell something? He took off his left shoe and handed me a twenty-dollar bill. He told me that these funds were to finance his Christmas eve snort of cognac, but he reasoned that Mike needed it more. This is a man that God is certain to welcome into heaven."

"So how much total?" *For what?*

"In two hours of good-natured pleading, I gathered six hundred fifty-one dollars and thirty-seven cents." *Silence in the room. Why?*

"That's not enough." *Dr. Hakeem.* "That's not nearly enough. We need at least five thousand to get him into the hospital."

"So…so that's it." *Nick. More silence. Then…very faint…perfume! Vanilla! Cookie! I can feel the warmth of her face! Her breath! She's right here with me!*

"Mike, I know you can hear me."

I can! I CAN HEAR YOU!!

"We're here. You're surrounded by your friends. You're going to make it. Hang in there. Be strong."

I'm so scared, Cookie. What's happening? Am I ever going to wake up?

"I'll stay with you."

He could feel her warm hand take hold of his. Magnus could feel himself starting to cry. Was he crying real tears? Could they see them? The sounds in the room began to fade: first 'O Holy Night' on the radio, then Nick and Dr. Hakeem and the Rev. Then Cookie.

Don't leave me.

But it was too late. Silence. Blackness. He wasn't as panicked as he was before. It was the hand, he could still feel the warmth of Cookie's hand. This time instead of resisting, he just let go and tumbled into the void.

CHAPTER EIGHTEEN

First, a sound. Very faint, and then louder. Was that…could it be "Jingle Bell Rock" by Bobby Helms? Lord almighty, he'd always hated that stupid song but now it sounded as sweet and glorious as Beethoven's "Ode to Joy." And then, an even greater miracle: light! First a kind of pulsing amber wash, and then flashing lights. These were blurry at first, then clearer. Christmas tree lights! Cookie's Christmas tree! And then Cookie herself sitting next to him, putting a washcloth on his forehead. She looked in his eyes and drew back, startled. "Mike?" Magnus blinked. "Mike, are you there? Can you hear me?"

Magnus swallowed. Will the words in his mind come out of his mouth? "Y-yes, I can hear you."

"Dr. Hakeem!" said Cookie. "He's awake!" Dr. Hakeem had been dozing in Cookie's cracked red

Naugahyde recliner. He bolted upright, grabbed his medical bag and bustled over. Cookie moved aside as Dr. Hakeem began by checking his eyes and ears. Then he took his vitals: blood pressure, heart rate, respiratory rate, and body temperature.

The beautiful faces of Cookie, Nick, and the Rev hovered just behind Dr. Hakeem as he asked Magnus, "How do you feel?"

He did a quick body scan. "I've got a headache, a bad one. Besides that…I guess I feel okay. Happy to be awake."

"Do you know where you are?"

"I think I'm in Cookie's apartment. Is that right?"

Dr. Hakeem smiled and nodded. "And can you tell us who you are?"

Magnus thought for a moment. *Well, this is as good a time as any.* "Yes. My name is Magnus Diller. I'm a multi-millionaire, number 187 on the Forbes list of the 400 richest people on earth. I have a 350-foot yacht, a twenty-acre mansion and my own private jet." The smiles turn to frowns.

Cookie shot an anxious look at Nick and leaned down to Dr. Hakeem. "He's hallucinating." *What?!?*

"Not uncommon. The shock to the brain was extreme." Dr. Hakeem was taking a large hypodermic needle out of his bag. "Mike, I'm going to give you a sedative. This will help you get a little bit more rest so you can feel better."

"No, really, I'm..." He felt a hot stabbing pain in his arm. "I'm fine, I don't need to...to..." and with that, the room began to fade. Instead of crying, Magnus began to laugh. Life is crazy. Crazy, crazy, crazy." And this time he didn't so much dive into that bottomless ebony pool of oblivion; he slowly lowered himself into it until he was fully immersed. Weightless. Gone.

CHAPTER NINETEEN

First, the sounds. *Music! What's that song?* Magnus focused. *"I met a man who lives in Tennessee, and he was headin' for Pennsylvania and some homemade pumpkin pie"…Perry Como, 'No Place Like Home For the Holidays'* Magnus smiled. *And voices!* He heard a thrum of conversation. *It's a party!* He opened his eyes and blinked. *Where am I?* Apparently, Cookie had moved him from her couch into her bedroom: a nightstand, a wicker basket of well-loved hardbacks (Rebecca Solnit, Margaret Atwood, Louise Erdrich), and one huge print on the wall: "The Flower Vendor" by Diego Rivera.

He sat up and winced. His forehead throbbed. This was the first time he'd been upright in, what? A day? Two days? Three? He'd lost track of time. Cookie had a full-length mirror on a stand. The mirror was canted upward, with hooks on the back of the stand for hanging tomorrow's wardrobe (or yesterday's). He pushed back the sheets, slowly rotated his torso, settled his feet on the floor and straightened up. So far so good! He did a body scan. Headache, about half as bad as yesterday. Ribs sore, legs sore, arms sore. Can he walk? He unbent himself and straightened his back. *Not bad.* He shuffled over to the mirror.

Magnus blanched at what he saw. He touched the over-sized gauze bandage on his head, with a blotch of red-brown blood seeping through the whiteness. His cheeks and chin were blighted with bum stubble. And these pajamas! A stained cotton t-shirt that said, "I Don't Do Mornings!" and pajama pants covered with cartoon images of "Grumpy," Snow White's seventh dwarf.

And all that fell away as Magnus's senses fully kicked in. He heard Andy Williams singing "The Most Wonderful Time of the Year" under the happy jabber of voices: Nick, Roxy, Cookie, the Rev, the Doc, Jazmin, Archie, the whole gang from the mall. And the smells! Hot butter and vanilla: Christmas cookies! Magnus considered his options. He could crawl back in bed and wait for the party to end, or...*What the hell...* He opened the door.

He blinked again as a wave of sound and light crashed over him. He staggered, but Nick was there to catch him. In an instant he was surrounded. Cheers! Hugs! Kisses! More hugs! *You're here! You made it! You look great! We're so glad to see you!* All this affection made him dizzy. Cookie sensed his distress and fended off the well-wishers. She led him over to a worn, food-stained armchair and plopped him down. He thought the chair looked familiar, especially the color. *Of course,* he thought. *IKEA. Ton of these in the office.*

Nick brought him a cup of coffee to go with the green-with-red-sprinkles Christmas tree sugar cookies that Cookie handed him. He was just about to take a bite when Jazmin dragged a chair from the kitchen table and plopped it next to him. "So glad to see you're up and about, Mike! How do you feel?"

"I'll give you two answers to that," he said. "Crappy, and thrilled."

"I bet," said Jazmin. "Is your name really Mike Dillon?"

SHIT. Alarm bells went off in his brain. "Uh, yeah, of course! Why would you ask that?"

"Because," said Nick, eavesdropping from an adjacent conversation, "When we were at the Emergency Room trying to get you help they told us your driver's license was a fake."

"And so was your Medicare card," said Jazmin.

Magnus tried to pull this memory out of the fog. *That's right. Shit.* "I haven't driven a car in years, so the license probably expired. And the Medicare card is…I don't know, it's probably, uhhh…" Something at the very back of his mind stirred the tiniest bit. He couldn't quite bring it into focus, but...

"Don't worry about, we'll straighten it out," said Jazmin. "Whoever you are..."

"I'm Mike Dillon!"

"So okay, Mike, how'd you like to become a very rich man?"

Magnus *almost* said, "I AM a very rich man!" but stopped himself. "I...ummm...sure, why not? How?"

"You, with me as your lawyer, are going to sue the damn mall," she said, black eyes blazing. "What they did to you is an outrage, and a crime. No security! None, the week before Christmas! Hoodlums running loose! Those guys just wailed on you! Slam dunk case!"

"Uh huh," said Magnus.

"And here's the best part," said Jazmin. "We'll finally find out who owns that dump. We'll blow past all those fake holding companies and find the real owners. We might end up owning it without paying a single red cent!" Magnus felt his stomach lurch. *Shit.*

"Yeah, sounds, ummm, good, Jazmin. Wow. Tell you what, can you let me think about it? Just for a day or two?"

She looked baffled. "What's to think about?"

Magnus tried looking pathetic, which wasn't at all hard. "It's just, I don't know, a really big step."

Finally, she smiled. "You think about it. Think about holding a check that had a six followed by five zeroes, which is your cut when we bank our cool million."

'Wow!" said Magnus. "That's more than I make…that's more…that's a lot of money!" Jazmin patted his arm and walked over to the cookie tray on the dining room table.

Magnus suddenly realized that, besides a sugar cookie, he hadn't eaten a bite of solid food in… well, however long he'd been out. He spied the usual lavish Cookie buffet: beef tenderloins in a mustard-cream sauce, sweet potato casserole, a broccoli-cheese dish, green beans with bacon, fresh biscuits…

"Can I make you a plate?" It was Cookie. She was already filling it with a serving spoonful of everything.

"I'd love that. Looks amazing."

"Glass of fruit punch to go with that?"

"Sure, yes, please," said Magnus. "And…I have a favor to ask."

"Sure," said Cookie. "What?"

"Could we find someplace to talk, like the kitchen or something? Just the two of us? There's something I want to know. It's kind of important, at least to me."

CHAPTER TWENTY

Cookie seated Magnus in the tiny breakfast nook behind the ancient refrigerator in the kitchen. More IKEA: a round table and two wobbly wooden chairs. She popped a pan of chocolate chip cookies into the oven and then sat herself down. As ravenous as Magnus was, he was even more curious. There was something he had to know. "First of all, Cookie, I…well, I just wanted to say thank you for everything."

"Everything? Like what?" said Cookie, puzzled.

"Like, you know, taking me to the emergency room, and then bringing me back to your place. Staying with me, nursing me back to health."

She smiled. "I'm just happy you're feeling better."

"I am, a lot," said Magnus. "The thing I'd like to know is, well, why did you do it?" Cookie stared at him. "I mean, I don't know…what was in it for you?"

Cookie's mouth started to move, and then stopped. She was struggling with his question. "What was in it for me…was to see you get better, Mike. I didn't do anything unusual. It's what people do. We're here to take care of each other." She paused, then added, "I mean, aren't we? Is there some other reason to be alive?"

Magnus felt a delicious twinge: that feeling he'd had watching Cookie love-bomb that girl who had lost her mother. He still hadn't drilled down as far as he wanted. He simply had to know for himself. "Yeah, I guess, but I mean…well…it's just that…"

"It's just that what?"

"It's just that, you know, there's no way I can pay you back."

Cookie looked mystified, like Magnus had said something in Burmese. "Pay me *back*?"

A feeling of mortification washed over Magnus. "Yeah. I mean, well…"

"You mean out of your many billions of dollars?" With that, they both burst out laughing.

"Yeah, I can't believe I said that out loud," said Magnus.

"You must have a rich inner life, pun intended," said Cookie.

"Oh, I do, I do." That twinge had lingered. It welled up every time he looked in Cookie's face. "I've...I've never met anyone like you, Cookie."

"What am I like?"

"You care about other people," said Magnus. "You're kind."

"Am I the first kind person you've ever met? In your entire life?" said Cookie, with a wry grin.

Magnus didn't smile. "Yes," he said. That stopped both of them for a moment. He saw a look in Cookie's eyes. Sadness? No. Worse. The look from earlier: pity. Magnus pressed on. "Are you...I know this is crazy, but...are you seeing anybody? Nick, maybe? Is there the slightest chance..."

Cookie put her finger on his lips to shush him. Then she got up, donned an oven mitt and checked the cookies. "Almost done. Another minute." She sat back down and looked in his eyes. "You're so sweet."

"No, really, I..."

"I'm not so good in the romance department, Mike." She looked past him, into a memory. "I told you my story. It just, I don't know, never seems to go well. So, I decided that falling in love was never going to happen for me. So I did the next best thing. I fell in love with my life. And I don't want to give up what I've fought so hard for."

Magnus felt like he had a hundred-pound barbell on his shoulders. *Why does it feel like I'm breaking up with the love of my life? I've never even dated this woman, barely know her!* "I understand, it was a stupid question…"

"No! Not at all! Look, maybe if you put your life together, in a couple of years, who knows? Life is full of surprises. Until then, let's be friends, okay?"

Magnus, heartbroken, looked at his hands as he nodded. She kissed him on the forehead, got up, and took the cookies out of the oven. She put one on a napkin and handed it to him. He took a bite, and had an out-of-body experience, it was that good. He watched himself eat that heavenly cookie, and then watched himself stifle tears. He was in heaven and hell at the same exact moment.

CHAPTER TWENTY-ONE

Nick burst into the kitchen, shattering Magnus's reverie. "Goddammit! Goddammit it to hell!"

'What is it?" said Cookie.

"Check this out," said Nick, handing her the smartphone. She read the screen and her mouth dropped open.

"What? Can they do this? They can't do this, can they?"

"E. Gerald Dudley can do any goddamn thing he wants, or at least he thinks he can."

"What did he do?" said Magnus. "What's going on?"

Nick took the phone back and read him the message. "Management of the Towne Center Mall wishes to alert all tenants that Michael Dillon has been terminated as mall Santa. Tomorrow a new Santa will assume the role of Santa Claus in

SantaVille. Please extend this new Santa every courtesy on what should be a busy Christmas Eve. E. Gerald Dudley, Supervising Manager of the Towne Center Mall."

"Fired!" said Nick. "On Christmas Eve! After having the living shit beat out of him because cheapskate Dudley wouldn't hire security cops!"

"C'mon," said Cookie, holding the plate of fresh cookies. "Let's go tell the others."

"I'd call Dudley a piece of garbage, but I'm afraid garbage would be offended," said Roxy. "So what are we going to do about it?"

"We could sue his ass," said Jazmin, "but we wouldn't get a court day until June."

"We could beseech heaven to rain down fire upon this miscreant," said the Reverend Luke Matthews. "Unfortunately, the Son of Man labors to save people's lives, not to destroy them."

"I think we should have a Santa Stand-Off," said Nick with a smile. "Like a sumo wrestling thing. We put both Santas inside a circle, and the one that bumps the other out of the circle with his stomach wins." Magnus laughed as he looked around. He was surrounded by friends, for the first time in his life.

"I say we make it our business to tell every parent in line what happened," said Archie. "Screw the new guy."

"That'd just make us look bad," said Nick. "Take away what little business we're going to get anyway."

A wet blanket of gloom settled over the group, mitigated only by bites of Cookie's latest master creation.

"I…I think I have an idea," said Magnus. "It's kind of crazy, but…

"But what?" said Nick.

"But even if it doesn't work it'd be a hell of a lot of fun," said Magnus.

"Fun? Sounds good to me, let's have some fun!" said Nick, with nods all around.

"It's going to take a little work….like we've pretty much got to start right now."

"So what are we waiting for?" said Roxy.

CHAPTER TWENTY-TWO

As Supervising Manager of the Towne Center Mall, E. Gerald Dudley had performed all kinds of unpleasant tasks that were not in his employment agreement. He had picked up trash, unclogged toilets, put out grease fires in the food court, and tried (with limited success) to quell rat infestations. He'd passed out discount coupons dressed as Uncle Sam on the Fourth of July, supervised a plastic egg hunt dressed as the Easter Bunny, and handed out chocolate kisses dressed as Cupid on Valentine's Day. (This latter role had the opposite effect of what he intended, driving away horrified young couples.) But he'd never summoned the fortitude to take on the one role that really scared him: Santa Claus. Dudley thought of himself as being as affable as the next guy, if the next guy was a bitter, driven workaholic whose superhuman efforts to keep this damn mall afloat were ignored by his corporate overlords. That said, the words "Dudley" and "jolly" had never been uttered in the same sentence.

That's why Dudley had fortified himself with several gulps of peach brandy before stepping out onto the Big Stage of the Towne Center Mall Grand Court. The Santa suit was a size too small so the trouser legs revealed his shiny white shins, and the black boots pinched his toes, but it was only for one day. God – and the makers of DeKuyper Brandy – willing, he could get through this.

As Dudley approached SantaVille, he noticed two things. First, there were no parents and children queued up in front of Santa's threadbare throne. Second, something was amiss with Sugar Plum. The elf was looking sweaty and pale. He flinched as Dudley strode up to him. "What?" Sugar Plum flicked his eyes over Dudley's shoulders in a way that filled him with foreboding. He slowly turned around. What he saw made his eyes bug out as his mouth dropped open.

What Dudley saw was a glorious, kludged-together DIY Santa set-up under a painted bedsheet that read, "THE REAL SANTAVILLE." This was a masterpiece of dumpster-dive "found" treasure, starting with Santa's "throne": the bucket seat of a 1968 Plymouth Roadrunner elevated on eight emerald green cinder blocks. The "SantaVille" behind Santa was a riot of garage sale plunder. PVC pipe candy canes were draped with burlap garlands festooned with chintzy red and green gift ribbon. There was a giant wreath made of wine corks. An eight-foot ladder had been painted cherry red, with particle board planks balanced on the steps. The planks groaned under a superabundance of small toys, snow globes, beanie babies and ornaments from Archie's toy shop. And directly behind Santa's head, the pièce de résistance: an iconic "Christmas tree" made up of two rusty handsaws glued together edge to edge, draped with a silver bicycle chain and topped with a silver tin foil "star."

The public was voting with its feet. Seven parents were standing in line, with kids who were ready to climb onto Santa's lap. Nick, in a green sport coat and peppermint-stripe bow tie, was handing out free cups of his delicious coffee, and Cookie was right behind him with her addictive bakery treats. Roxy, Louise and Jazmin, dressed in homemade elf costumes, were circulating in the center mall court herding more parents into line. Archie was directly behind Santa dressed as Frosty the Snowman, and the Reverend Luke was…what was he? A snow-white "hair-hat" sat on his head, with an attached white beard, all topped with a Burger King cardboard crown. He wore red pajamas under a white luxury hotel bathrobe held in place by braided gold cord. In his hands, a bowl filled with milk chocolate coins wrapped in gold foil. Ah yes, of course: Melchior the Wise Man, lavisher of gifts on the baby Jesus, offering each child a coin as they exited.

Dudley wasn't going to take this lying down. This was a treason! A slap in the face, a rebellion designed to degrade his authority. He and he alone was the official, authorized, one-and-only Towne Center Mall Santa Claus. He thought about calling the police, having these interlopers hauled off to the gray-bar hotel. But no. The thing to do, Dudley decided, was to go mano-a-mano with these mutineers. He'd put up with crap like this his entire life. This time he'd fight. And just as he made that decision, he heard a deep, booming "HO HO HO!" Could that be…Mike? Had the spirit of the real Santa Claus somehow inhabited the body of Mike Dillon? And in that moment, Dudley knew it was hopeless. He'd reached into his Christmas stocking and grabbed a great big lump of coal.

That night on the local television news, "Dueling Santas at Local Mall!" was the perfect Christmas Eve kicker story. Viewers saw "SantaVille II" overrun by swarms of giggling youngsters, while the original SantaVille looked like WhoVille after the Grinch had picked it clean. Turns out the first parents that morning had called their friends, and soon hundreds of people in the neighborhood wanted to get a load of the North Pole ThunderDome: "Two Santas Enter, One Santa Leaves." The report featured interviews with parents, kids, Sugar Plum (Dudley eventually gave up and let him join the winning team) and finally Magnus, who couldn't stop bellowing "HO HO HO!" At first, Magnus wondered if he should let himself be captured for a TV news report, but then he figured the white beard and Santa hat would protect his identity…and, frankly, he was so happy, he was past caring about his old life. Something had changed. No way could he go back to the way things were. He wasn't sure what his next move was, but Magnus "Killer" Diller was dead. Cookie had killed the Killer with kindness, and in his place…well, Magnus was enjoying the process of figuring that out.

CHAPTER TWENTY-THREE

The employee break room of the Towne Center Mall had never been so merry. The gang had plopped Santa's muscle car "throne" on top of the steel-frame picnic table in the center of the room, along with the most-loved of the zany DIY decorations. Someone had wrapped the decrepit vending machine with the lights they'd stripped from that wretched excuse for a Christmas tree in the center of the mall. The lights seemed to blink in rhythm to Nick's smartphone playlist of pop Christmas hits from the '50s and '60s. Nick was handing out disposable plastic champagne flutes. "The bag describes these things as 'elegant drinkware,'" he cackled as he filled the flutes with screw-top sparkling wine. Right behind him, Cookie carried a tray of pink Italian "champagne cookies" with red and green sprinkles. Magnus thought he was through being amazed at Cookie's ingenuity in the kitchen, but a cookie that could stand up to champagne? Yes, she'd done it. She was a goddess, come to earth to bring about world peace through cookies. Wow.

Roxy and Louise were frugging to the Phil Spector/Ronettes version of "Sleigh Ride." Dr. Hakeem and Jazmin were even more boisterous, freelancing steps that mixed faux-martial arts moves with square dance do-si-dos. Archie said something that made the Reverend Luke howl with laughter. And Magnus? He was perched on his muscle car bucket seat Santa throne chasing those scrumptious cookies with that tepid, caustic sparkling wine and basking in this…this what? *This new life*. Yes, it was a new life. He didn't know where this new life would take him, but he knew he could never go back to the empty, fear-driven law-of-the-jungle rat race he'd left behind. *I can stop running. There is no saber-tooth cat chasing me.* He smiled as he thought, *I'd rather be here than any place else in the world, even New Zealand. Sorry, Brandi.*

Dudley stuck his head in the door. Everyone froze for a single second, until Nick yelled, "Dudley! Get your bad self in here, you old rascal!" As a hesitant Dudley tiptoed inside, he was group-hugged by the high and happy party goers. Somebody handed him a plastic flute, Nick filled it, and Cookie popped a cookie in his mouth.

"So, Dudley!" said Roxy. "What about Santa here? Is this guy a kid magnet? A rock star? Is he or is he not the best Santa this stinking hell-hole has ever had?"

"The *best*?" Dudley blanched, and everyone hooted with laughter.

"C'mon, Dudley, admit it! This is this the best Christmas eve this dump has had in the last ten years," said Nick. Everyone looked at Dudley, who was finishing his second cookie and reaching for a third.

"Well," he said. "It pains me to say so…but, yeah. I guess it was." A big cheer went up.

"Any doubt you'll keep the dueling Santas gimmick for next Christmas?" said Jazmin.

"I don't know about that," said Dudley, who then looked at Magnus. Magnus could see him struggle, and then smirk. "Okay, yeah, Mike did alright. He went from godawful to halfway decent in record time…thanks to you folks propping him up." *Amen to that,* thought Magnus.

More dancing. More sparkling wine. More cookies. More laughter. And then Dudley revealed the reason he came to the break room. "You all know the mall is going to be closed for Christmas," he said. "Well, I figured after everything we've gone through this month, what if we had a little Christmas party for ourselves? Like around 11 a.m., in the center court?"

"Oooh, yes!" said Cookie. "And let's do a Secret Santa gift exchange!"

"Secret Santa?" said Dudley. "What's that?"

"I'll write everybody's name on a napkin. We'll put the napkins in Mike's Santa hat. You choose a name, and you get to be that person's secret Santa!"

Secret Santa. Magnus had an idea. *I'll have to call Fletcher to clear it, but that wouldn't be a problem, because it's my mall.* He smiled. He had just figured out the perfect way to step into his new life. His eyes settled on Cookie, who was helping Nick pass out cups of coffee. *You, my dearest one, are in for a really big surprise.*

"Sounds fun!" said Nick. "We should put some kind of dollar limit on the gifts. What do you think? Ten dollars? Twenty?"

"Let's make it ten," said Cookie, busy scrawling names on napkins. "The less you spend, the more imagination you have to put into it."

"I'd happily settle for a couple of your million-dollar chocolate chip cookies," said Roxy.

CHAPTER TWENTY-FOUR

Dudley unlocked the door to the employee's entrance at 10:33 the next morning, and Magnus was right behind him. Magnus's gift was in an envelope in his back pocket. He wanted to linger a few minutes in the center court: just look around at the place and try to imagine what it might become if these people made it over to their own liking. He saw Nick open up his shop to make coffee for the party. Nick waved hello. "Hey! You're early!"

Magnus smiled and walked over to him. He started to say something but the coffee grinder drowned him out as it pulverized the beans. After he was sure Nick was done he said, "So, Nick, what do you think about Cookie's plan to buy this place? Turn it into some kind of, I don't know, 'community center' or something?"

Nick chuckled. "I love the woman. She's the nicest genius I know."

"Amen to that," said Magnus.

"But she's not…oh, what's the word…I guess 'practical' is pretty close. She's a dreamer. She thinks everything should have a happy ending. And this place…" He stopped, looked around.

"What about it?" said Magnus.

"You can see it yourself, Mike," said Nick. "This place hasn't got a chance. It's coughing up blood. I'd be amazed if we didn't get our butts kicked out of here next year, maybe even next month. The people that own this place don't give a damn about us. They're going to sell it, tear it down and build condos or something. Amazed they haven't done it already."

"Uh huh. What'll you do then?"

"Are you kidding?" said Nick. "You think people are going to stop buying coffee? It's America's legal addiction, liquid go-faster, the workingman's friend. If everything goes to hell and I can't get somebody to lease me space for a new shop, there are fifteen thousand, one hundred and forty-nine Starbucks locations in America. I'll have a job in twenty minutes. It's Cookie I'm worried about."

"Worried? Why?"

Nick was surprised that Magnus had to ask. "You've tasted her cookies. That lady should be a millionaire with her recipe box and her baking skills. And here she is, stuck in this dump. Just between the two of us...." Nick motioned Magnus to lean in, even though no one else was around. "She's barely breaking even. She doesn't charge enough, and she gives away half her cookies to little kids and homeless folks. If we all get the boot...well...I'm not sure Cookie would have the grubstake to start over. I'm afraid she might sell her cookie recipes for a buck fifty, or even give them away."

Before Magnus could reply, Nick looked up and shouted, "MERRY CHRISTMAS!" Magnus turned his head: the rest of the gang was headed toward that pitiful, dead-brown Christmas tree in the center court of the mall. "Your special Merry Christmas cup of Nick's Holiday Blend, which is Nick's Everyday Blend with Cinnamon, is on its way over there!" And with that he handed two four-cup coffee carriers to Magnus and grabbed two more himself.

CHAPTER TWENTY-FIVE

As the group waited for Dudley to arrive, Magnus looked around him. Sure, it was the same broken-down jumble of distressed, homemade hovels he'd mocked a couple of days ago…but today the whole place seemed to shine. It was illuminated by the spirit of his new friends, who got out of bed every single day and came here to fight it out on the battlefield of American free enterprise. He looked at Cookie, who was taking the gifts and arranging them under the tree. Cookie. He loved Cookie. He was *in love with* Cookie. And very soon, he knew there was a very good chance that Cookie would be in love with Magnus Diller. And that made him smile.

Dudley arrived. As Magnus expected, Dudley offered the smallest possible nod to Christmas: a sprig of fake holly pinned to his wrinkled windbreaker. Sugar Plum appointed himself "Secret Santa's Helper" and started passing out gifts.

Nick gave Jazmin a desk sign that said "Jazmin Monroe – Towne Center Community Co-Op President" Jazmin hugged him as Cookie said, "That's the spirit! We can do this thing!"

Louise gave her partner Roxy the most hideous Christmas sweater ever created. The front featured a reclining (naked) cartoon Santa in front of a tree, with his bag of goodies strategically placed in front of his mid-section. The words said, "I have a Great Big Package for You!" Roxy burst out laughing and tried it on. "Luckily, it's five sizes too big, so I could wear it as a dress…if I wore dresses."

Jazmin gave Sugar Plum (real name: Lance Kroger) a rare vinyl copy of The Ethel Merman Disco Album, which reduced him to a puddle of grateful tears. He almost knocked her over jumping into her arms to thank her. "I've always wondered if I was the love child of Ethel Merman and Ernie Borgnine," he said. "This is just…just so perfect. Thank you."

Dr. Hakeem gave Archie a coupon for a free prostate exam, which got a big laugh from everyone, especially Archie. That's because Dr. Hakeem gave everybody free exams for everything.

Archie gave Reverend Luke a certificate, redeemable anytime, for ten sinners to be delivered to The First Storefront Church of Jesus Christ, Troublemaker. They both understood the reference to "Guys and Dolls," but Luke told Archie he was going to hold him to his promise. Archie said it wouldn't be hard to make good considering the neighborhood they were in.

Dudley gave Nick what was by far the largest gift under the tree. Nick unwrapped it. It was a prosthetic leg. "That thing's been sitting in lost and found for a least five years," said Dudley.

Nick didn't know what to say. Did dour, dumpy Dudley have a spectacular sense of humor he'd been hiding all these years, or was it…just Dudley being Dudley? Nick said, "Well, I was hoping for a bag of reindeer farts, but this is next best thing."

Roxy said, "I'm Dudley's Secret Santa, but his gift isn't under the tree."

"Where is it?" said Dudley.

She turned toward the mattress store. "Diego! Get your ass out here!" Diego pushed aside the sheet of plywood blocking the door. Roxy said, "Your gift is your new best friend Diego. You're going to lay off the kid, because we love him and he's helping us and it's the Christmas thing to do and if you want to rat him out, you'll have to go through us. Capiche?" All eyes turned toward Dudley. His eyes darted from Diego to Roxy to Nick. The gang grouped together in a kind of defensive line guarding Diego.

Dudley's body slumped. He was beaten. Then he amazed everyone by saying, "Yeah, okay. It's

Christmas, what the hell." He walked over and hugged the kid, who, after a long moment, hugged him back." Roxy and Louise then produced a Star Wars backpack filled with gently used YA paperback sci-fi novels and gave it to Diego. He hugged every single person around the tree, including Dudley for a second time.

Sugar Plum gave Louise a CBD Bath Bomb. "It'll mellow you right out, get your whole body stoned. Throw it in a hot bath and bring along some deep-fried Oreos."

Cookie gave Magnus a basket filled with frosted gingerbread cookies: nine reindeer cookies (yes, Rudolph had a red nose), Santa, Mrs. Santa, Santa's sleigh and six elves. Magnus grinned as he held them up one by one. Gasps, cheers, applause. "We can't eat these," said Nick. "They're too…too beautiful." Every head nodded.

Cookie scoffed. She walked over, picked up Santa, and bit his head off. "They're cookies, people. Cookies are for eating, especially when they're fresh. And these go great with coffee." That set off a dash for the basket. Two minutes later all Magnus had left in his basket was a single gingerbread elf. He didn't mind, as he'd already gobbled Rudolph. Scrumptious, of course.

"So, are we good?" said Sugar Plum. "Everybody happy?"

"Wait a minute!" said Reverend Luke. "Mike, look in your basket, under the napkin." Magnus lifted the green linen napkin…and saw a pile of dollar bills. "Six hundred fifty-one dollars and thirty-seven cents, Mike. The money we collected to get you into the hospital. It's a down payment for your new job as Mall Greeter."

Cookie said, "And Easter Bunny!"

Nick said, "And next year's Santa." He turned to Dudley. "You good with that, Dudley?

Dudley said, "Well, he's got his first week's salary, we'll see how he works out…"

"C'mon Dudley, give it up," said Nick. "Play nice. Lie if you have to."

"Okay, okay." He turned to Magnus. "Just don't screw up."

Sugar Plum said, "Okay, I guess that's it…"

"What about Cookie?" said Louise. "Who got her name?" They all looked at each other.

"That would be me," said Magnus. He reached into his back pocket and pulled out an envelope. Then he walked over to Cookie and handed it to her.

She looked at him, puzzled. "What is it?"

"Open it and find out." As Cookie did this, Magnus brought out the other envelopes and handed them to Nick, Roxy, Archie, Jazmin, Dr. Hakeem, and Reverend Luke.

Cookie scanned the page. "I…I don't understand."

"According to this," said Nick, "Wait a minute…it says here that you own this place. And…and you're giving it to us?"

"That's right," said Magnus. "Remember what I said when I came out of my coma? That my name was Magnus Diller…"

"Ahhh! The multi-millionaire!" said Nick. "Number…what was it…"

"187."

"Right, 187 on the Forbes list of the 400 richest people on earth!"

"With a big yacht!!" said Dr. Hakeem.

"And your own private jet!" said the Reverend.

"Uh huh," said Magnus. "And everybody thought I was hallucinating." He saw them look at each other. They still thought he was hallucinating.

"Mike," said Cookie, "we may not believe you, but we believe *in* you."

"I appreciate that, Cookie," said Magnus. "But the thing is, I am Magnus Diller. I'm the Chairman and CEO of Opportunity Investments. We own real estate developments all over world, as well as twelve shopping malls. This is the only one that isn't making money. I came here on a bet." He turned to Dudley. "You're the only one who got it right."

"I did?" Dudley was in shock.

"You thought I was a spy from corporate. I was! I was going to prove that you lovely folks had formed a conspiracy to drive the value of this place so low that you could buy it yourselves for next to nothing. It never occurred to me…well, a lot of things never occurred to me: that I could be so wrong. That folks could be happy without much money. That people would take care of other people for no other reason than…than…" He looked at Cookie. "It's what people do. We're here to take care of each other." He looked away from Cookie, back at the group. "I was the dumbest of all dumb guys: the dumb guy who mistakes himself for a genius. Well, you folks wised me up. The least I can do is give you this damn place so you can turn it into…" He looked at Cookie. "Whatever you want it to be."

"Thank you, Mike," said Cookie.

"Magnus."

"Er, right. Magnus. That's such a lovely story. And if you really could give us this place, that would be incredibly generous of you. So you see, it doesn't really make any difference who you are."

"He IS who he says he is!" A voice echoed through the empty mall. Magnus turned his head and reeled backwards in shock. *Dwayne? And Fletcher? What the hell?*

"My name is Dwayne Babcock. I'm a junior partner at Opportunity Investments. This is my associate, Fletcher Skowron. He's our legal counsel." Dwayne walked over to Magnus and put his arm around his shoulder. He turned to the group. "I'm here to deliver some very good news…and some news you may not like so much."

"Good news is always welcome," said Reverend Luke.

"The good news is that this is, indeed, Magnus 'Killer' Diller, owner of this mall. He is, in fact, one of the richest men on the planet. And he does, as of this moment, have the power to give you worthy folks this struggling enterprise."

"So, what's the bad news?" said Magnus. He was over the shock. Now a sickening realization was turning his stomach.

Fletcher unzipped his brown leather portfolio and pulled out a sheaf of papers. He said, "The bad news is that you almost certainly won't retain that ownership for any length of time." He handed the papers to Magnus.

"You see," said Dwayne, "the ownership covenant you signed last year has a 'Consideration of Corporate Competence' statute."

"The sanity clause," muttered Magnus.

"That's right," said Dwayne. "By giving away a valued corporate asset, especially in light of a pending sale of like assets, without consulting your executive board members or legal counsel, you are no longer mentally competent to run said enterprise."

Suddenly Magnus could see the whole thing, it was beautiful. He turned to Dwayne. "You practically dared me to come here. Because…"

"Because it proved you were losing it. I was just trying to win the damn bet. I never imagined you'd give this place away. That's the cherry on the parfait. Thank you so much for that."

Magnus smiled. It was just the kind of scheme he'd have dreamed up. "Tell me. Those kids. Did you send them to beat me up?" Dwayne just smiled at that. Magnus walked over and, to Dwayne's surprise, stuck out his hand. "Nicely played, Dwayne, I've trained you well."

"Thanks, I guess."

Magnus turned to Fletcher. "I am a little surprised that you…"

Before he could finish, Fletcher said, "I was with you at the very beginning, Magnus. I should have been cut in for half of everything. You screwed me, old buddy. And now it's payback time. Nothing personal."

"No, of course not," said Magnus. A long moment of silence as he pondered what to say next. He looked straight at Cookie as he said to Dwayne, "Listen, a lot has changed over the last few days, more than you know. Any chance we can make a deal?"

"Like what?" said Dwayne.

"Like we create a plan where I step away from the company. I become, I don't know, some kind of honorary Chairman Emeritus or something. Dwayne, you become the new CEO, with Fletcher as your Chief Operating Officer and co-owner."

Magnus could tell from Dwayne's smile that he'd anticipated this play. "We want it all, boss. This is graduation day from Magnus University. Let me see if I can remember those words on the final exam. Oh yes. 'Show no mercy. Take every dollar. For me to win, you have to lose. Well, guess what, boss. You lose."

"Well, okay then," said Magnus, smiling. "I guess I'll see you in court."

PART THREE

CHAPTER TWENTY-SIX

The Courthouse was an Art Moderne masterpiece built by the WPA in 1937. This building told the people of the country that the government had righted itself. Americans designed this, built it out of American marble, granite and limestone, and filled the courtrooms with dark walnut wainscot panels that rose ten feet up the walls. Magnus sat at one table, with Jazmin next to him as his attorney. Behind him sat the mall gang: Cookie, Nick, Roxy, Louise, Diego, Archie, Dr. Hakeem and Reverend Luke.

At the other table, Dwayne scrolled through emails on his smartphone while Fletcher made final notations to his opening arguments. At precisely 10 a.m., Judge Judith Hunsacker entered, welcomed everyone, gaveled the proceedings to order, and invited Fletcher to give his opening statement.

"Your Honor," said Fletcher, "I sincerely wish we were not here. I have been an associate – and until recently, a friend – of Magnus Diller. I was with him at the beginning. I watched him build his company into a mighty leviathan of world commerce. He became one of the wealthiest, most successful people in the world."

Magnus whispered to Jazmin, "Here comes the 'but then.'"

"But then, your Honor, I started to notice something that…well, it made me sad. As so often happens with people who achieve great success, Magnus started to spend less and less time on the business and more and more time finding creative ways to indulge himself. A modest suburban home became a lavish mansion with a three-hole golf course in the backyard. He used company funds to purchase ever bigger yachts and then private jet aircraft. I was troubled by this, but I found myself making excuses for him. Was he the warmest boss in the world? No. Did he sometimes treat his executive partners with disdain bordering on contempt? Yes, that was true as well. But it was his money! Nobody out-worked Magnus Diller, he had earned his success. But then…"

Jazmin shoved her legal pad over to Magnus. She'd written, "Here's where you lose your mind." Magnus scrawled, "I'll miss myself. So sad."

"But then I began to notice little things," said Dwayne. "Judge Hunsacker, it might be useful to mention that my mother suffered from dementia for the five years before she passed away. I was her caretaker so I became attuned to the symptoms. Magnus began to forget names, and where he'd put things. That made him angry. And then he became – and I'm fully aware of the implications of this charge, your Honor – he became paranoid. Mister Diller spent eleven million corporate dollars on what he himself called a "luxury survival bunker" in New Zealand. Why New Zealand? Because Mr. Diller obsessively researched the safest place to live in case of a worldwide calamity, like a nuclear holocaust or a financial meltdown or a pandemic. He was getting ready to spend last year's Christmas holiday there until he became obsessed with the idea that the poor, pitiful souls with those bedraggled shops in the Towne Center Mall had entered into a conspiracy to defraud him."

Fletcher turned toward the Judge and stood directly in front of her. "We know something happened during the few days he pursued this mission, going undercover as the mall's Santa Claus. He was brutally attacked by some young toughs. He was in a coma for two days. We have a Doctor who is willing to testify that Mister Diller's cranial trauma made the on-set of his dementia worse. This is when he committed the act that affirmed he could no longer be trusted to guide the destiny of a major corporate institution."

Fletcher stepped away from the Judge and brought the full measure of his rhetorical gifts to bear on his ending statement. "Mr. Diller took what belonged to the company and, without any advice or consultation as to the ramifications of his actions, gave this asset to the very people he was convinced were ripping him off only days before. There is only one reasonable and just verdict this court can render: that Magnus Diller be stripped of his corporate responsibilities and removed from his duties as leader of Opportunity Investments as per the 'Consideration of Corporate Competence' statute in our charter."

The Judge invited Jazmin to give her opening statement. It was short and sweet. "This hearing is about a very simple question: Does being generous make you crazy, or a good human being?" She returned to her seat.

Now the hearing moved into the witness phase. Fletcher called Dwayne as a witness. Yes, he was Magnus's closest colleague and personal sounding board. Then, reluctantly (as if), he described his mentor's fragile mental state as he embarked on his undercover mission. "I knew he'd be better off with his paramour…"

"The pole dancer? Brandi Foxx? With two x's?" said Fletcher.

"That's right. He'd be better off in New Zealand with her than he would be going undercover in this derelict shopping mall. But he just couldn't be persuaded. He'd gone undercover once before and proved that some tenants were ripping him off to lower the value of a property he owned. He was positive this was an even more heinous version of the same thing. He alone could uncover this plot. And then he was going to get them. Put them in jail. Destroy them. It got pretty dark, truth be told. Not the kind of thing you wanted to hear the week of Christmas."

"When you speak of the corporate enterprise, exactly what was at risk here?"

Dwayne pretended to ponder this. "Opportunity Investments, with all its properties, employs about three thousand people. The lives of these people depend on a stable, responsible management team."

"And you believe that Mr. Diller has put those jobs – the jobs of three thousand people – at risk?"

Dwayne looked at the ground, then up, sadly, at the man he loved so much. Magnus couldn't help but smile. Here's another skill he'd given Dwayne: the ability of a sociopath to feign empathy on demand for personal gain.

"I do, Mister Skowron. I can't tell you how sad it makes me. This man taught me everything..."

"No shit," whispered Magnus, causing Jazmin to chortle.

"…and now, to see him suffer this decline, to spiral into madness…" Dwayne bowed his head, shielding his face from the Judge. The people in the room could hear a small sob. After a long moment he raised his head and, eyes glistening, and looked at Fletcher. "I've thought a lot about the best way to handle this. I think that saving all those jobs is important, but…" He looked at Magnus. "I think it's also the best thing for Mister Diller. He can finally get the help he needs."

After a short break, Jazmin got her shot at Dwayne. "Mister Babcock, the course of action that Mr. Diller initiated – giving away the mall – isn't that basically the same course of action you advocated before all this began? Didn't you just want to get this property off the books of Opportunity Investments?"

"Yes, that's right. I mean, I wanted to sell the Towne Center Mall at what everyone knew was a giveaway price."

"So Mister Diller's actions here essentially align with yours," said Jazmin. "He's just getting this worthless property off the books so that your company can make a five hundred and fifty-two-million-dollar deal, realizing a profit of sixty-eight million dollars."

"That's exactly right." Both Jazmin and Magnus were baffled by Dwayne's composure. He was smiling, calm. He acted as if he were the prime witness for the defense.

"And according to the bet you made with Mister Diller, since there was no plot, you and your compatriots will split that sixty-eight million dollars five ways, realizing a personal gain of thirteen point eight million dollars apiece."

"Yes. Plus we will each get six weeks of vacation next year and use of the personal jet for one of those vacations."

"And yet, despite this ridiculous windfall…"

"OBJECTION, your honor. This was an honorable wager entered into by both parties in good faith."

"Objection sustained," said the Judge.

Jazmin pressed on. "And yet, despite this, ummm…let us say generous payout, you want to destroy the man who created the very company that made this wager possible…who built the company and hired you and your compatriots…and who, as founder and Chief Executive Officer, has every right to distribute the assets of said company as he wished."

"Yes, I do," said Dwayne.

"Why?" said Jazmin.

Dwayne once again shifted to an expression of compassionate anguish. "Ms. Monroe, I was closer to Mr. Diller than anyone else. He confided in me, shared his thoughts, his fears…and his dreams."

Uh oh. Magnus knew something was coming. Something big. Something bad.

"Mr. Diller called Mr. Skowron and myself on Christmas Eve to tell us of his plans to give the mall to his new friends. Isn't that right, Magnus?"

Magnus, surprised at being addressed from the stand, said, "That's right."

Dwayne looked back to Jazmin. "He sounded...well, different. Both Fletcher and I could hear something strange in his voice. He had changed somehow. He was a little...I don't know...I guess you'd say 'loopy.' He told us that he wanted to give away this particular mall...and something more."

This is it. The payoff. Dwayne looked at Magnus. "He said he wanted to give away all the assets of our company. For free. Because that's what Santa does. That would make everyone happy. That's when we knew we had to take action."

CHAPTER TWENTY-SEVEN

Magnus picked up the best cookie in the world – the first Cookie cookie he'd ever tasted, his favorite, a chocolate chipper – and took a bite. He felt the same thrill he felt that first time: the separate flavors flowing together, the hint of salt pushing against the sugar, and a rich, melty chocolate chip in each and every bite. What could be better? Just a sip of Nick's special blend coffee. He surveyed the dour faces of his friends. He felt none of their misery. How could he be upset living in a world filled with cookies this good?

The rest of the gang was hunkered down with him in a scarred and scuffed up wood-paneled meeting room, picking at lukewarm take-out Chinese food that looked even less appealing under the crackling fluorescent tube lights. Nobody had said a word during the lunch break.

Finally, Nick stood up and pulled a sheaf of papers out of his front pants pocket. "Here you go, Magnus."

Magnus took the papers: the shares in the mall. Nick said, "That's what's causing all this brouhaha. When we go back in there, you can give them to your colleagues and we can forget this whole business."

Magnus pushed the shares toward the center of the table. "Thanks, everyone, but that won't change anything. And the fact is, I'm happy I gave you that mall. I consider it the best thing I've ever done: maybe the only really good thing I've ever done."

"You could lose your whole business!" said Cookie.

"Magnus 'Killer' Diller is the one they're after, but Magnus 'Killer' Diller died on Cookie's couch. He was killed with kindness. Everything he had, everything he was, everything he wanted died with him. None of that means anything to the man who is sitting here with you enjoying the hell out of this astounding chocolate chip cookie."

"So, who is my client in this proceeding?" asked Jazmin.

"Mike Dillon," said Magnus. "And Mike Dillon has a question for you."

"What's that?" said Cookie.

"If I get my butt kicked in there, as it kinda sorta looks like I'm gonna," he said, "Can I really come back and work with you folks? Is that Mall Greeter position still open?"

Cookie looked at Nick, then at the others. Smiles. "Yeah," she said, "I think we can work something out."

CHAPTER TWENTY-EIGHT

They were back in court, and Dwayne was back on the stand. Magnus looked at his former acolyte and detected just the tiniest bit of smugness creeping into his demeanor of earnest concern. As Jazmin stepped toward Dwayne, Magnus stood up. "If it please the court, your Honor, may I be heard?" Everyone turned to him in surprise, including Jazmin, who looked a question at him, as in 'what the hell?"

"What is it, Mister Diller?"

"I have a long-standing, if complex relationship with Mister Babcock. I believe that we can wrap this entire proceeding up if you'll grant me permission to engage in a dialogue with him."

"Your honor, I object," said Fletcher. "Mr. Diller has no standing in this court..."

"No, no," said Dwayne, smiling. "It's fine, Fletcher. We can talk this out."

The Judge looked at Dwayne, then at Magnus. "Well, this is highly unconventional, but if Mr. Babcock agrees with Mr. Diller that we can expedite this matter…"

"I do, your Honor," said Dwayne. Now Magnus smiled. He could tell by the look on Dwayne's face that his disciple was ready to deal the final, killing blow. He was ready to step over the body of his mentor to assume the throne, with all its perks and privileges. The king was dead, long live the king.

Magnus stepped around the table toward Dwayne, passing Jazmin who whispered, "Hope you know what you're doing."

"Me too," whispered Magnus.

Magnus sketched the arc of their relationship: from mentor/acolyte to boss/assistant and then master partner/junior partner, with Magnus grooming Dwayne to take over the business when the boss finally retired. "Is that about right?" he asked Dwayne.

"Yes, that's correct."

"Now, Dwayne, if you win in your effort to invoke the 'sanity clause' and I'm judged incompetent to run my own company, how much money will you and your colleagues take charge of?"

"About three and half billion dollars."

"And what will I be left with?"

Another smile, this one so small only Magnus could see it. "Well, you structured the company so that just about everything you've got is in the company's name – your cars, the jet, your estate – so…I guess the answer is not much."

"Nothing, in fact."

"If you say so," said Dwayne.

Magnus turned to the gang in the courtroom. "Actually, If I lose, I'll walk away with nothing but the love, goodwill and affection of my new friends. I'll walk away with nothing but a light heart and a bounce in my step and a reason to get up in the morning. And tomorrow morning I will wake up knowing in my heart what it feels like to be loved and accepted, something I never had all the years I ran Opportunity Investments."

He turned back to Dwayne. "So there's no need to worry about me. I'm in great shape here, Dwayne! If I win I win, and if I lose I win. So with the court's permission, I'd like to make you a settlement offer."

For the very first time in the entire proceeding, Dwayne looked baffled. He looked at Fletcher, who shrugged. *Why not?* "Sure, okay, I guess," he said.

Magnus felt something he hadn't felt in a while: that delightful mini-rush of adrenaline he'd get when he was about to close a deal by setting a trap for his prey. Only this time, there was no corrosive taint of hostility in the surge, just the edge he'd feel from a great cup of coffee. "So here's the offer, Dwayne. You drop this action, and I walk away from the company. You and Fletcher and the Brain Trust get Opportunity Investments. That includes three billion plus in corporate assets, the company jet, the yacht…I'll even throw in the New Zealand luxury survival bunker."

"Sounds good," said Dwayne. "So what do you get?"

"All I want…is eighty thousand dollars."

"Eighty thousand?" said Dwayne, unable to conceal his surprise.

"That's what my friends and I need for the ten percent down payment on the Towne Center Mall, which you will then sell to us, getting it off your books so you can realize a profit of sixty-eight million dollars on the mall sale. Will you make that deal, Dwayne? This is it. The last time you will ever have to deal with Magnus Diller. Make this deal, I'll be out of your life forever."

He could see Dwayne's back stiffen, and his face cloud with malice. *I trained you,* thought Magnus, *because I knew you were the one would go all the way, just like me. Now I'll find out if I was right.*

Dwayne closed his eyes to calm himself. Then he flashed a cobra-like smile and said the words he'd been waiting to say for five years. "Sorry, Magnus. This time we win. And for us to win, you have to lose. We get everything, you get nothing. Nothing."

Magnus smiled. *I was right.* Then he nodded at Cookie and turned to the Judge. "Well, you heard it yourself, Judge. You heard the deal he just turned down. So the question is…" He turned and looked at Dwayne. "…which one of us is really crazy?"

CHAPTER TWENTY-NINE

Can something be both crazy and the most natural thing in the world? Magnus pondered this as if it were a zen koan, an unsolvable riddle designed to break his mind wide open. Here he was in the new corporate headquarters of Opportunity Investments – what used to be an outpost of the Dream Cloud Mattress Company, inside the Towne Center Mall – about to call his new Board of Directors to order. And the whole set up was, well, both crazy and the most natural thing in the world.

Yes, he'd won the case. The Judge ruled that you don't have to be insane to share your good fortune with others. And then Magnus had completed the mall deal, shut down the corporate office and cleaned house by giving generous buy-outs to Dwayne, Fletcher and the other Brain

Trusters. The idea of petty revenge died with his previous incarnation.

Magnus appointed a new Board of Directors: Cookie, Nick, Roxy, Louise, Jazmin, Dr. Hakeem, and Archie. Together, they had turned Towne Center Mall into the Towne Community Center with a three-doctor free clinic, a full-service legal clinic, a gym, a yoga studio, a farmer's market and a "pay-what-you-like" gourmet mess hall with seven different kinds of ethnic cuisine. This all complemented the expansive new stores selling cookies, coffee, toys and new and used books. Every month the Center hosted a celebration, with concerts and special events. February was a favorite, with a Valentine's Day Sadie Hawkins Hoe-Down, every girl grab a partner and dance to a live polka band. November wasn't bad either: a month of giving thanks, with free meals for everyone, along with a smile and a hug.

This new manifestation of Opportunity Investments had then rescued nineteen other distressed malls in struggling urban areas and turned them into community centers. Every single one of them was losing money, which meant that, if the company couldn't turn them around, OI would be flat broke…in seven hundred and eighty-one years.

All these new community centers featured Cookie's Cookies, which were also available on-line, in gourmet food stores, and as the featured comestible at Grindhouse Coffee. Cookie's

Cookies would be a major profit source of the company if the CBO (Chief Baking Officer) didn't insist on giving away as many cookies as she sold. She did so by order of Magnus Diller, who was the company's CEO, loyal customer and husband of the CBO.

Diego was corporate director of IT, so everything ran smoothly, thank you.

Oh, back to those month-long celebrations. What about Christmas? Every Christmas Magnus would put on the Santa suit and welcome children of the community. This was Archie's favorite month, because happy parents would walk right from SantaVille into his store where he'd make the dreams of their children come true.

And on Christmas Day, Secret Santa time, the gang would gather around that spectacular 30-foot Douglas fir and hold hands as the Reverend Luke Matthews said the blessing:

"Dear Lord, dear God, dear Heavenly Oneness: Well, we made it through another year. Bless us and keep us this Christmas in the spirit of infinite love and generosity as we remember that the very best gifts in this life are friends, family and loved ones. Fill us with the spirit of your son, our Savior and Lord Jesus Christ and remind us in every moment of every day that we are what you are doing here on planet earth."

And then, as everyone else began chattering and hugging and eating cookies and sipping coffee, Magnus would stand back and marvel at how far he'd come. When he spent his days wholly focused on trying to make money, he felt unhappy, desperate and driven by fear. Now that he spent his days giving it away…well, he felt like he was the richest man on earth. *Does that make me crazy?* He thought. *Yeah. It does.* And he picked up a cookie and joined the celebration.

THE END

ABOUT THE AUTHOR

R. Lee Procter understands the power that stories have to change lives. He's studied timeless tales of transformation like *A Christmas Carol* and *It's a Wonderful Life*. These stories invite us on an emotional journey to the lives we were born to live: joyous, generous, loving and beautiful. Procter has worked in advertising, television and as an Imagineer for the Walt Disney Company. His previous novel, *Sugarball*, told the astonishing-and-true story of Negro League baseball players almost losing their lives in the Dominican Republic in 1937, only to find their place in baseball history as "the best of the best." *Sanity Clause* is Procter's latest: a timeless tale as bright as the star on top of the tree, and satisfying as homemade hot chocolate on a cold winter night.

Claude Monet Designs
Yankee Stadium
A Love Story
R. Lee Procter

NOTE FROM R. LEE PROCTER

Word-of-mouth is crucial for any author to succeed. If you enjoyed *Sanity Clause*, please leave a review online — anywhere you are able. Even if it's just a sentence or two. It would make all the difference and would be very much appreciated.

Thanks!
R. Lee Procter

We hope you enjoyed reading this title from:

BLACK ROSE
writing™

www.blackrosewriting.com

Subscribe to our mailing list – *The Rosevine* – and receive
FREE books, daily deals, and stay current with news about
upcoming releases and our hottest authors.
Scan the QR code below to sign up.

Already a subscriber? Please accept a sincere thank you for
being a fan of Black Rose Writing authors.

View other Black Rose Writing titles at
www.blackrosewriting.com/books and use promo
code
PRINT to receive a **20% discount** when purchasing.

www.ingramcontent.com/pod-product-compliance
Lightning Source LLC
Chambersburg PA
CBHW030858200726

48289CB00003B/805